Moonlight Harvest

Other books by Edward Lodi

Ghosts from King Philip's War

Nantucket Sleigh-Ride: A Notebook of Nautical Expressions

Deep Meadow Bog: Memoirs of a Cape Cod Childhood

Cranberry Chronicles: A Book About A Bog

Forty-one Walnut Street: A Journal of the Seasons

Cranberry Gothic: Tales of Horror, Fantasy, and the Macabre

Shapes That Haunt New England: The Collected Ghost Stories of Edward Lodi

The Haunted Violin: True New England Ghost Stories

Haunters of the Dusk: A Gathering of New England Ghosts

The Haunted Pram: And Other True New England Ghost Stories

Murder on the Bogs: And Other Tales of Mystery and Suspense

Ida, the Gift-Wrapping Clydesdale: A Book of Humorous Verse

The Ghost in the Gazebo: An Anthology of New England Ghost Stories
(editor)

Witches of Plymouth County: And Other New England Sorceries

Witches and Widdershins: A Modern-day Witch Story

The Old, Peculiar House: Ghost Stories Read by the Author
(one-hour audio on CD)

MOONLIGHT HARVEST

Haunted Cranberry Bogs
of
Cape Cod and Plymouth County

Edward Lodi

ROCK VILLAGE
PUBLISHING

Middleborough, Massachusetts

Rock Village Publishing
41 Walnut Street
Middleborough MA 02346
(508) 946-4738

Lodi

Acknowledgments

The following is a publication history of the stories included in this collection:

"The Grayness of Ghosts": *All Hallows*, June, 2006

"Chomp": no previous publication

"Joe Baker Stops By": *Prime Time Cape Cod*, May 2003;
The Haunted Violin, 2005

"The Bogman's Tale": *The Haunted Violin*, 2005

"The Old House by the Bog": *Cranberry Gothic*, 2002

"Cousin Bertram's Story": *Haunters of the Dusk*, 2001;
The Old, Peculiar House (audio CD), 2002

"The Face in the Ditch": *Cranberry Gothic*, 2002

"Tortuga": *Cranberry Gothic*, 2002

"Oh Danny Boy": *Nuclear Fiction*, Nov / Dec 1990 issue;
Shapes That Haunt New England, 2000

"King Philip's Ghost": *Deep Meadow Bog*, 1999;
Ghosts from King Philip's War, 2006

"A Gift for Halloween": *Deep Meadow Bog*, 1999;
Haunters of the Dusk, 2001

"Moonlight Harvest": *The Haunted Pram*, 2002

"Murder on the Bogs": *Murder on the Bogs*, 2001

"Flume Child": *Elegia*, Vol.1, No.3, 1992;
Shapes That Haunt New England, 2000

"Mock Turtle Soup": *Over My Dead Body!*, December, 1999;
Murder on the Bogs, 2001

"The Haunted Screenhouse": no previous publication

"Petal on a Wet, Black Bough": *White Knuckles*, Spring, 1995;
Shapes That Haunt New England, 2000

This book is dedicated to two poets named

Christopher:

Christopher Bursk

and

Christopher Conlon

Whether based on actual hauntings, legends, or oral traditions, the stories in *Moonlight Harvest* are presented as works of fiction, and the characters portrayed are fictitious. Any resemblance of any of the characters depicted in the stories to living persons is entirely coincidental.

Likewise, the photographs in *Moonlight Harvest* are generic; their purpose is to suggest typical scenes associated with cranberry bogs in southeastern Massachusetts. They do not represent specific locales mentioned or implied in the text.

Table of Contents

Moonlight Harvest

Preface

It is luckier for a ghost to be vividly imagined than dully "experienced;"

and nobody knows better than a ghost how hard it is to put

him or her into words shadowy yet transparent enough.

—Edith Wharton,

The Ghost Stories of Edith Wharton

BESIDES FEATURING AN ARRAY OF APPARITIONS, dastardly deeds, and macabre happenings, the seventeen ghost stories collected together in *Moonlight Harvest* share one other characteristic: they all take place on the cranberry bogs of Cape Cod and Plymouth County.

Most are set in the not too distant past, when the region was far more rural than it is now—though even today there are many isolated spots in southeastern Massachusetts that constitute ideal settings for ghost stories: dense swamps, deep woods, remote lakes and ponds, lonely pine barrens, wind-swept fields, with not a soul (a *living* soul) for miles around.

This is familiar turf. I know cranberry bogs well. I've written two books of memoirs about growing up near the bogs and working on them: *Deep Meadow Bog* and *Cranberry Chronicles*. In my youth I spent many a lonely day, and even lonelier nights (during frost season) toiling away with only an occasional fox or snake or deer for company. And I've experienced a ghost or two.

However, *Moonlight Harvest* is not intended as a guide book to the region's haunted cranberry bogs. Within these pages you won't find any maps or explicit directions on how to reach specific locations, nor have I identified any of the bogs by name. (All personal and many place names appearing in this book are wholly fictitious.) Few cranberry growers would appreciate spook hunters, thrill seekers, or the idly curious tramping up and down their property in hopes of seeing or perhaps even photographing a ghost. Therefore, I have not revealed the exact locations of any of the hauntings, which in most instances were one-time events or, if recurring, were only temporary in nature and have long since ceased. It is doubtful whether Joe Baker still "stops by," or whether an inchoate black mass still forms on frost nights on a certain wooden bridge somewhere on Cape Cod. Hopefully, those particular ghosts have been duly laid to rest. And of course, several of the stories are only loosely based on fact; whatever real-life bogs inspired those tales may have been, to begin with, haunted more in the figurative than the literal sense. "Flume Child," for example, falls into this latter category.

⋙⋘

Some time ago I wrote a book of true New England ghost stories which included as an afterword an essay titled "The Ghost Wars (Fact Versus Fiction)." In it I attempted to explain why, although I appreciate both fictional and factual ghost stories, I have a definite preference for the former. Having compiled this present collection, which includes a variety of ghosts, some "real," some "imagined," and not a few "in between," I have thought it prudent to repeat some of the ideas presented in that essay, to move those ideas from the back of that book to the beginning of this one, and to supplement them with additional musings on the matter.

And so, without further ado:

"Are these stories true?"

How many hundreds—nay, how many thousands—of times have I been asked that annoying question!

Annoying, because of the implications: "If these stories are *not* true, then why have you wasted your time writing them? And why should I, a seeker after truth, waste my time reading them?"

Or something to that effect.

No one ever asks Stephen King—one of the most prolific, popular, and best-selling authors of all time—whether *his* stories are true. Perhaps that's because he had the good sense, from the very outset, to label his fiction "horror" or "fantasy" rather than "ghost stories."

Factual ghost stories have their devoted following, as do made-up ghost stories. And never the twain shall meet. Or so it seems. Actually I write both: stories that are absolutely true, and stories that are little more than fig-ments of my (some might say over-active) imagination. I enjoy writing—and reading—both genre, and have included examples of each in this volume.

Moreover, one or two of the so-called fictional stories have their genesis in legends, half-whispered tales, told decades ago to a group of frightened youngsters huddled for warmth and mutual comfort around a smoldering stove deep in the woods on the edge of a swamp in southeastern Massachusetts. The truth of those particular phantoms—the absolute faith with which the reality of their existence was accepted—is indelible and undeniable.

Fact or fiction? If I had my druthers—if I had to choose only one—it would be fictional over factual, for reading and for writing. A well-crafted ghost story—whether by a recognized master such as M.R. James, E.F. Benson, H. Russell Wakefield, Edith Wharton, or (dare I say it?) my humble self—has the power to evoke all those familiar, archetypal clichés that readers or listeners so perversely love: chills running up and down the spine, frame wracked by shivers of unbearable apprehension, breath held in dread anticipation.

Hark! What is that rasping against the window pane? That creaking on the stairway? That shadow against the wall? Is someone—some*thing*—lurking behind the curtain? What is that mournful sound, so like an anguished moan, that seems to originate in the closet? And why does the dog cringe in abject terror at the foot of the bed?

A loaf of bread, a jug of wine, and a ghastly tale read by the flickering flames of a smoldering fire: what greater contentment can life—or, for that matter, the afterlife—offer?

Why then—if I am so fond of fabricated tales—do I bother to write *true* ghost stories? Before I attempt to answer that question let me explain why I—and millions like me—find ghost stories (of any stripe) so appealing.

Fondness for ghost stories can be attributed to the universal appeal of being scared. Life, as we know, presents many terrors that are all too real: dangers or tragedies which can instill within us feelings of utter helplessness. Ghost stories offer us a way to escape these feelings: an opportunity to be scared while at the same time feeling snugly safe.

For many of us, no doubt, this fondness has something to do with early exposure. I recall episodes from my own childhood: those autumn evenings when, huddled together in the shadows of a darkened room in an isolated shack deep in the woods, my buddies and I listened to creepy tales we knew couldn't be true—could they? We fervently hoped they were not. After all, home for all of us, to one extent or another, was a long, lonely bicycle ride away.

Being scared yet ultimately emerging unscathed offers assurances that life is manageable, that we can cope with and conquer our fears.

Fine. But (going back full circle) why prefer fictional over factual?

Well, for one thing, many true ghost stories are not really *stories*. They are eye-witness accounts, or reportings. They lack a plot: a beginning, a middle, and an end. They may also lack suspense. For example, someone glances up from reading a newspaper and sees the ghost of Uncle Archie—who died in his sleep and was peaceably buried five years ago—sitting in his favorite rocking chair. Then Uncle Archie abruptly vanishes.

That's it. That's the complete "story." It may be a frightening experience for the person who sees the ghost. Or of great interest to those who personally knew Uncle Archie. But for the rest of us, the incident's appeal is merely in its mystery. Geewhilikens! Did someone really see a ghost? Can such things be? Or did the person reading the newspaper just imagine the whole thing? We ponder a moment, shrug our shoulders, then turn our minds to other matters.

But a fictional ghost story—skillfully narrated—may cause us to sit on the edge of our seat as our hair bristles and goose pimples sprout all over our body. Can anyone who has read "Oh Whistle, And I'll Come to You, My Lad" ever forget the experience? M. R. James's classic story not only is scary—it scared me out of my wits the first time I read it—but it also serves as a cautionary tale. Don't mess around with or treat lightly things that are beyond your ken, for you may live to regret it.

Writers of fiction enjoy freedoms which are not always available to writers of nonfiction. Fiction writers are free to manipulate, to delve into the minds of characters, to give their imaginations free range. For example, in a story (not included in this volume) written a number of years ago and inspired by an abandoned stone quarry that lies on conservation land not far from where I live, I employed the literary equivalent of slight of hand; there is indeed a ghost, but not the one the reader expects. Hopefully, along with a twinge of fear, by stringing the reader along for a while I've also provided an element of pleasurable surprise.

In "Flume Child," included in this present volume, (a story which many readers have told me is very scary), I present the action from the point of view of the ghost—who insists all along that she's not really dead: After all, "There ain't no such things as ghosts. I'm flesh and blood, same as you." But we know better. (There's another story in this collection related from the perspective of the ghost—one who likewise doesn't realize that he or she is dead—but that's a surprise I won't spoil now by telling you which tale I'm referring to.)

True ghost stories can be every much as effective, i.e., *scary*, as those that are made-up. This is especially the case if the ghost is perceived as malevolent. Look to "Cousin Bertram's Story" in this volume for an entity that may be neutral, but is more likely (judging by its actions) overtly evil. Moreover, there is always that added element in a true ghost story: the knowledge that this really happened, and could conceivably happen again— to you or me.

In *Haunters of the Dusk*, my first book of true ghost stories, I stressed that the more certain I was that a story was true, the more likely I was to present it in journalistic fashion. But the more skeptical I was, the more likely I was to use the techniques of fiction.

Moonlight Harvest deviates from that dictum; all of the stories, true or not, are presented as if they were works of fiction. I've used all the literary devices at my disposal, including, but not limited to: plot manipulation, dialogue, characterization, point of view, diction and what not. That is to say, I've done my darnedest to make these stories entertaining.

The Grayness of Ghosts

When visible, ghosts may present themselves in a spectrum of
colors. Monks and nuns in ruined abbeys seem to favor brown.
Throughout the ages witnesses have seen, on occasion, spectral ladies
draped in green, or purple, or scarlet; or gentlemen wearing red or yellow-
striped trousers; or children outfitted in pink or blue. But the vast
majority of ghosts come in gray.

O N THE FIRST EVENING IN MARCH a group of friends sat by the hearth of a roaring fire in a log house in southeastern Massachusetts. The previous week a nor'easter had blanketed the area with two feet of snow. Drenching rains followed, with only partial melting before a deep freeze set in, resulting in an ice pack that gripped the earth like a vise.

"Normally I wouldn't light the fireplace when it's this cold outside," the host was explaining. "There's too much heat loss up the chimney afterwards. But it's so seldom we get together like this, I figured, why not?" He tossed a hunk of seasoned oak onto the fire, made adjustments with the poker, and strolled over to the front door. Idly, he switched on the exterior lights and peered through the glass. "Hey, look, a fox!"

The others hastened to the windows. Beyond the porch a small, vaguely feline shape hovered in the shadows by the frozen bird bath. As they watched, it stepped forth, bringing into profile a long, pointed muzzle. It stood a moment to cast a quizzical glance at the blazing lantern on a post by the driveway, tilting its head from side to side as if mesmerized by the brightness, then began to back off. Bushy tail horizontal to the ground, it turned quickly from the circle of light and disappeared into the woods.

"Beautiful!" a woman named Laura said, just before the fox vanished. "Was it a she—a vixen? She didn't look like other foxes I've seen. It's not a coyote?"

"A gray fox," her host explained. "I've seen her before. She comes by to scavenge under the bird feeders for corn and nuts—and I imagine any rodents she might happen upon."

"Charlie, did you see her?" Laura inquired of her husband, who had come to the window and stood briefly by her side, but had almost immediately returned to a position next to the hearth.

He replied with a nod, but stared into the fire as if lost in thought.

"Well," Laura demanded, annoyed by his inattention, "what did you think of her? I don't believe I've ever seen a wild creature quite so beautiful. I don't know—so graceful, yet so fragile. Ephemeral perhaps is what I mean?"

"Like the grayness of a ghost," her husband said.

"Well, yes," Laura said, grudgingly. "But are ghosts actually gray?"

"You two are having a strange conversation," their host remarked.

"Charlie's a strange man." Laura sighed, not without affection. "I suppose that's why I married him. He's anything but ordinary."

Charles withdrew his gaze from the fire. "I don't know why I said that. 'Like the grayness of a ghost.'"

"What's all this about ghosts?" a blowzy, heavyset woman asked. "Let's not talk about ghosts. Who believes in them anyway?"

"Why *did* you say that, about ghosts?" Laura asked, later, as she and Charles were driving home.

"Oh, something I came across the other day. An old manuscript buried among some papers I acquired at an estate sale. Seeing the fox reminded me of it."

"Can I see it?"

"It's at the shop. I'll bring it home tomorrow."

Though the next day was Sunday, normally a busy day on Cape Cod for those antique shops along Route 6A that remain open off season, the fierce cold kept customers away and Charles returned home early. He remembered the manuscript and handed it to Laura in a manila envelope as he entered the house. She put it aside to read later.

When, after supper, they went into the living room, she took the envelope and opened it. "It's handwritten," she observed as she slid the loose sheaf of papers onto her lap.

"That's why I was so long in getting around to looking at it," Charles said. "I've had it kicking around the shop for at least a year. Don't ask me which estate sale it came from. I don't remember."

"At least it's not musty," Laura said, as she arranged the yellowed sheets in a pile on the floor next to her. There were twenty sheets all told, unlined, with writing in blue ink on both sides, and each page numbered, though there was no title nor author's signature. The manuscript simply began at the top of page one and continued on to the end of page forty, in a neat though somewhat crimped, apparently feminine, hand.

She picked up the first sheet and began to read:

✍

I remember hearing my parents talk of Jeremiah Bumpus and reading about his "tragic misadventure" in the New Bedford *Standard-Times*. Normally I wouldn't have opened a newspaper (other than to read the funnies) but the whole town was talking about the accident and I knew the family, though at that time only slightly.

A cranberry grower, Jeremiah Bumpus lived with his family in a house he himself had built on upland next to their bog. The mishap occurred one frost night, in the fall, when Jeremiah was clearing the trash rack at his pump house. The rotted flooring gave way under his weight, and he fell into the pump shaft and was killed—horribly mangled by the propeller blade, though the newspaper didn't go into gory details. But we could imagine what condition the body must have been in, since (being out for frost, which sometimes required staying out most of the night) he wasn't missed until the next morning and had been in the shaft for hours, though people said that the propeller must have jammed, stalling the motor before he was ground up too badly. In any event, the funeral was closed-casket. (I don't know why I dwell on this, except to contemplate the horror of it, and the anguish his family must have felt.)

The obituary mentioned that he left a wife and two children: a stepson, Ronald Eldredge, age twelve, and a daughter, Shirley, age nine. I remember the children's ages because Shirley was a classmate of mine.

Everyone expected (this was the gossip in town)...everyone expected Jeremiah's widow to sell the house and bog and move back to Maine where she hailed from (and where her first husband, Ronald's father, had been a lobsterman; he too had died tragically, drowned in Penobscot Bay). But Hannah Bumpus defied expectations and stayed on, relying on hired help to raise and harvest her cranberries until her son grew old enough to take over.

Which he did—but just barely. Ten years after the death of her second husband, tragedy struck once more: Hannah's son, Ronald, age twenty-two, was found lying in the woods, dead of a gunshot wound to the head.

I heard the news on the radio; I remember thinking, what an unlucky family! The *Standard-Times* reported the death as accidental. The official finding was that Ronald Eldredge had tripped as he stepped over a stone wall while carrying a loaded shotgun. But those of us who grow up in New England know that tripping with a loaded gun over a stone wall is a time-honored means of committing suicide—sufficiently ambiguous to leave room for doubt (important in the early days, when those who died by their own hand not only brought disgrace upon their families but were denied burial on hallowed ground)—and I had my suspicions. From what little I knew of him, Ronald was a strange, quiet boy who kept to himself and had few, if any, friends.

Just exactly how Ronald Eldredge died was none of my business, of course—except that two years later things happened that made it my business.

This all came about because of the Great Depression. I was twenty-one, no longer willing to live at home with my parents—who, I felt, treated me more like a child than the adult I considered myself to be. Meanwhile Hannah and Shirley Bumpus were in need of a hired hand, but could offer only room and board in lieu of wages. As two women living alone—and isolated—they made it known that they preferred that their live-in help be female. But I wonder—given the dark history of her household—the tragic deaths of two husbands and a son—did Hannah Bumpus feel that any male who joined it might be jinxed—might suffer a similar fate? Anyhow, I heard about the job, applied in person, and was hired.

I moved in the next day.

The house, a one-and-a half-story Cape, had three bedrooms, the largest, Mrs. Bumpus's, was on the first floor, the other two upstairs. Mrs. Bumpus left unsaid what was obvious: that the bedroom I was to occupy had been her son's. No doubt the cot had been his as well, along with the small oak desk and chair. The bedspread and curtains, too frilly for a male, were probably spares from Shirley's room.

One of the dormered windows in the bedroom that was now mine overlooked the cranberry bog with its sunken fields crisscrossed by dikes and irrigation ditches, and beyond: the reservoir, the swamp, and the sur-rounding uplands.

It was a wild, desolate scene—or so I thought, used as I was to living in town, close to people, with all the amenities (necessities?) such as electricity, a telephone, and indoor plumbing. Needless to say the Bumpuses were not "hooked up." The cost of introducing telephone poles and electric wires (not to mention town water or sewerage) to such an out of the way location was far beyond their means.

But I soon adjusted. The workday was long and arduous; by the time dusk came around I was tuckered out, longing for my soft, comfortable bed, so had little need for candles or oil lamps. In warm weather the outhouse was a minor inconvenience. (What it might be like in winter was something I'd worry about when the time came.) I did not miss having a telephone, since there was no one I especially wanted to talk to. As for a radio—we had one that was battery operated, and though we used it sparingly, a half hour perhaps each evening, it did keep us in touch so to speak with the rest of the world.

I have always been affected, if only in a minor way, by the full moon. Is it the reversal of the norm, the mutation of night into day—the absence of soothing darkness—that disturbs my sleep? Or something deeper-rooted from human prehistory, when our primitive ancestors, crouching in fear, fell prey to nocturnal predators? Whatever the reason, on nights of the full moon I have trouble falling asleep; what sleep I do achieve is fitful, so that when I awake (usually in the predawn) it is with my nightdress hopelessly rumpled, my bedclothes all in a tangle—as if in tossing and turning I wrestled with a thousand demons.

It was on such a night in June, just a few weeks after I moved in, that I found myself wide awake and pacing the floor. Knowing that sleep would elude me, possibly for hours, I dragged the chair from the desk and positioned it by the window, where the light pouring in enabled me to sit and read. (These being hard times, when all were called upon to sacrifice, I was reluctant to light a lamp; I did not wish to consume more oil than I felt entitled to.)

I don't recall what book it was I read, just that it failed to hold my interest. My gaze soon wandered, within the room at first, onto the patterns of moonglow that lay on the floor like marble slabs, then out the window and onto the scene below. I have heard moonlight described in liquid terms, as if it were fluid: lying in "pools" or "splashing" against a wall. But that June night its phosphorescence seemed harsh, frozen, the objects trapped within its beams sculpted, as if chipped from solid blocks.

With the book lying face down on my lap I sat and contemplated the view. The fields of vines, with their networks of dikes and irrigation ditches, lay naked and exposed, like the segmented floor of an ancient sea. From the edges of the woods the trees—oaks, and maples, and tall, lonesome pines—cast long ragged shadows. Beyond the bog the surface of the reservoir glinted like a placid lake. Everything was still, the only movement the faint stirrings by a westerly breeze of lilac leaves in the shrubbery immediately beneath my window.

Restive, I enjoyed as best I could the quietude and the sweet perfume of the lilacs. I thought of home, and my parents—and felt ashamed that I did not miss them more.

Only gradually did I become aware that there was something—a shape, some sort of figure—moving along one of the dikes. Initially I thought it must be an optical illusion, a figment created by gazing too long onto the pallid landscape. But then I saw it distinctly: a human form, though whether male or female, child or adult, I couldn't ascertain.

Setting the book aside I slid from the chair to crouch with my elbows on the sill. The figure left the dike and began moving along the shore, toward the house, though still too far away to be easily discerned.

Child, surely—though lacking perspective against that moon-bleached background I couldn't be absolutely certain. Male, no doubt of that, dressed as he was in shirt and dungarees. But there was something else, something peculiar. The child…the boy…blended too readily into the background. That odd circumstance was due, came the realization—along with a shudder—to his absolute lack of color. Even in a nighttime world fully furbished by the moon most objects retain some color. But not this figure, which—lacking all hue—was a solid washed-out gray. *And cast no shadow.*

I shrank from the window.

Next morning Mrs. Bumpus's accustomed knock failed to waken me; to do so she had to enter the room and gently shake me by the shoulder while speaking my name.

"We're working you too hard," she said, half jokingly, when I came down to breakfast.

"Oh, no," I assured her. "It's just that I sleep badly when there's a full moon. I was wide awake till long after midnight."

As indeed I had been. But solely because of the moon?

Had I seen a ghost? Had I seen *anything*? Or was that which I thought I saw nothing more than the figment of a disturbed dream? Crouching by the window, watching…something…as it approached the house: that much

I remembered. But then—exhausted by long days of physical labor—I must have fallen asleep. And crawled back into bed? It didn't make sense, especially in the light of day.

And so I dismissed it from my mind.

That evening, right after supper, with mumbled apologies to Mrs. Bumpus and her daughter I dragged myself upstairs to bed. Shirley and I had spent the better part of the day under a broiling sun yanking weeds from a section of newly planted vines: ten hours of monotonous, back-breaking toil the result of which, if past experience was any guide, would be a sound night's sleep. And sure enough, despite the sultry air I fell into a dreamless sleep as soon as my head hit the pillow—only to waken abruptly some time later in a state of vague unease. Not owning a watch, and with no clock in the room, I had no idea of the exact hour, though, as on the previous night, moonlight flooded the room. On this occasion, however, it was not the moon that drew me to the window but thoughts—and fears—of what I might see, outside on the bog, creeping toward the house.

At first I saw nothing save a leprous landscape as devoid of movement as it was of color, with not even a faint rustling of lilac leaves to ease the sense of utter solitude. I was about to pull my aching body away from the windowsill and return to bed, and what I hoped would be peaceful slumber, when once more I detected...movement...on the dike. It was movement without form, if that be possible. Only gradually did it take shape, become manifest, and then I saw that it was the boy, the lad I should say, since he appeared to be at least ten, possibly older. As before he left the dike and began to make his way toward the house.

Spellbound, in a dreamlike trance I knelt by the window—though I knew full well this was no dream. The unease that roused me from sleep had grown into something greater—akin to fear, terror even, yet at the same time I felt a certain calmness, a resolve to remain steadfast.

The figure moved slowly, deliberately, along the dirt track that bordered the bog. As it approached I saw that there could be no mistake regarding its nature. It was something...otherworldly—a ghost—no doubt of that. Yet it appeared neither wispy nor transparent. On the contrary it looked solid—as solid as the gray, wet clay it seemed (though of course could not be) composed of.

Curiosity kept me glued to the windowsill, and fear. As the specter neared the house it entered an oblong patch of shadows cast by a grove of elms and disappeared, swallowed by absolute darkness. I suddenly felt myself breathing as if for the first time since waking, as if all along I had been holding my breath. It will not emerge, I told myself. It will not emerge. It has shown itself—for whatever purpose—only to return whence it came.

But emerge it did, closer to the house now. Yet even as it stepped forth from the shadows it slowed down, only to halt beneath my window, with its feet planted firmly on the ground—as if all the while it had known of my presence. As it tilted its head back to cast a glance upwards its eyes stared directly into mine.

Like a sleeper enmeshed in nightmare I felt paralyzed. Unable to move I shrieked—a silent, inward shriek. I wanted to tear myself away from the window, to crawl across the floor and cower in a corner, but something compelled me to remain: something—despite my fear—born of my own volition.

In the end I could have turned my back on that terrible gray specter; I could have lifted myself from the sill and walked away, pretending it was all a dream. But I chose not to. Or some power deep within me chose not to. He was, after all, but a boy. A boy not of this earth perhaps; but nonetheless a boy. A young lad. Was it maternal instinct that kept me there? Or—some inkling of the awful truth?

Something of both perhaps.

As his gaze rose up and met mine he nodded as if in acknowledgment of my...concern? my...involvement? Or was it a nod of recognition? Despite his ghastly pallor he somehow looked familiar—as if he were a boy I knew or had once known. *Did* I know that sad gray face, that flaxen, curly hair?

He beckoned, motioning with his arm, as if he wished me to come down and join him. But of course I did not, I could not, I dared not. A look of anguish crossed his face, as if he understood, and although he continued his upward glance he faded, gradually, his grayness merging, dissolving, into pale moonlight.

The next day I felt—and no doubt looked and acted—like a zombie. Once again Mrs. Bumpus had to enter my room in order to waken me from the exhausted sleep into which I had eventually lapsed. At breakfast she kindly suggested that I take the day off from my labors and rest, but I insisted on working as usual.

How I longed to confide in her—and in her daughter, for whom I was beginning to feel the affections of a sister. But I could not, for a variety of reasons. Pride, for one. How could I tell them that I had seen—twice—a ghost? Moreover, that it had attempted to communicate. Would they believe me? Would they doubt my sanity, or at least my common sense? Would they suggest that perhaps I was unfit for the rough life of a bog worker, a life of hard toil and isolation? That I was suffering from over-work, a case of nerves? That perhaps I might be better off back living with my parents, performing work more suitable for a woman?

And then there was my concern for them. Had Mrs. Bumpus not suffered enough, from the tragic death of first one husband, then another, and of her only son? And Shirley, from the loss of a father and a brother? How could I broach to two dear women, who had endured so much, and been so kind to me, the morbid subject of a ghostly apparition?

Miraculously I got through the day, another ten hours of stooping and kneeling under the blistering sun, and once again I headed straight for bed as soon as the supper dishes were done. I both longed for, and dreaded, sleep. Fatigued—both physically and emotionally—I did not know my own mind. Did I, or did I not, fervently wish to see the little gray boy again?

I fell asleep and awoke as before and went to the window and saw him again, though this time less distinctly; he appeared on the dike but vanished almost immediately afterwards. On the next night, too, I saw him—this time even more a phantom. The following night not at all. And I understood: his strength waxed and waned with the moon.

That summer I led a Jekyll and Hyde existence. For most of the time I was Dr. Jekyll, that is to say, my normal, everyday self. But on nights of the full moon, in July and August, I became Mr. Hyde, taking my stance by the window, watching for, seeing—and being seen by—the little gray specter. And each time our eyes met he beckoned, pleading— by his de-meanor and the anguished expression on his colorless face—for me to come down and join him. But I was afraid.

How long this dual existence, this secret life, this dark night of the soul might have gone on, I cannot say. On nights of the full moon I was like one mesmerized. And yet by late August I had considerably tough-ened, both bodily and mentally; loss of sleep on those nights when I stood watch no longer affected my physical stamina, nor during the day did I exhibit "nerves." Outwardly I was a healthy, robust twenty-one-year-old.

Perhaps eventually, on my own, I would have answered the little boy's call, would have obeyed his summons, and leaving my post by the window gone down and taken his hand.

But in the end I did not have to do so, alone.

By the latter part of August work on the bog had slowed. All the dikes were mowed. (Under Shirley's tutelage I had learned to operate the tractor—and, so far, had managed not to tip over on the steep banks.) Harmful insects were under control; the vines fertilized; wooden boxes stacked in neat pyramids, ready for the harvest that would begin some time after Labor Day. For the first time that summer there was opportunity for leisure.

One Saturday evening, as a special treat before the commencement of harvest, Shirley and I borrowed her mother's car and went to a dance in Onset. We did not return to "the bog" until well after midnight, long past our usual bedtime. The next day, to recuperate, we slept late and remained home while Mrs. Bumpus attended church before going on to visit friends in a neighboring town. She would not be back until late afternoon.

Shirley and I spent an hour or two lounging in the shade of the elms before a sudden shower drove us indoors. We retreated to the parlor, where I picked up a magazine and sitting on the sofa began to flip lazily through its pages. On the seat next to me there lay a leather-bound photo album.

"Ma must've been looking through it last night while we were at the dance," Shirley said, when she noticed the album. "She looks at it sometimes when she's feeling lonely. Of course it only makes her sadder, seeing pictures of my dad, and Ronnie."

She sat next to me and resting the album on her knees opened it. Politely, I set down the magazine and peered over her shoulder. The earlier photographs, sepia toned, presented their subjects in stilted, formal poses. Shirley skipped rapidly over these, but paused when she came to a section of more recent snapshots.

As she turned the pages one of the photos caused me to inhale sharply. "Who's that?" I blurted out, staring at a photograph of the spectral boy—or his spitting image.

"Why, my brother Ronnie of course." She looked at me oddly.

"But…" I lifted my eyes toward a grouping of framed pictures, which included that of the young man I knew to be Ronald, prominently displayed on a corner shelf.

Shirley followed my gaze. "The photo in the album is of Ronnie when he was a young boy. About twelve. It was taken just before my dad died. Here's one of me taken around the same time. I was only nine," she added, with a note of sadness.

Of course! How could I have been so obtuse, not to have recognized Ronnie.

"But it doesn't make sense!"

"What doesn't make sense?" I must have turned pale, for she took my hand in hers. "You seem ill. Is there something wrong?"

I shook my head. Then, unable to contain myself any longer, I told her of the spectral boy that stood under my window beckoning on moon-lit nights.

It took her a while to absorb the full purport of my words. Finally she said: "But my brother was not a little boy of twelve when he had his accident. He was a man of twenty-two. It can't be *his* ghost that you see."

"But it is," I insisted. "If that's your brother's picture in the album, then it's his ghost I've been seeing."

Just then a car pulled into the yard. "Ma's home." Shirley looked at me with imploring eyes.

"I won't breathe a word of this to your mom," I promised, and we let the matter rest until later, when under the pretense of desiring fresh air after the storm Shirley and I took an evening stroll around the bog.

"This is the dike where I first see him," I remarked as we approached from the side farthest from the house. "I'll be gazing out into the night and…suddenly…he's just there, always in the same spot—roughly the middle—heading toward shore. He never runs, or stops to rest, or turns to look right or left, but keeps on at a steady pace until he reaches the spot under my window. Oh, and if in the morning I check for footprints there are never any there."

"What can it all mean?"

"You do believe me?"

"Of course! That is, you wouldn't make it up, and if you were dreaming the whole thing you'd know it."

Then and there we resolved to get to the bottom of it.

"The next full moon isn't until September the tenth," I said. "It's best if we wait till then. You can come to my room well before midnight and…" I shrugged, letting my words trail off.

Harvest began the following week. A crew of ten or twelve men and women—Portuguese mostly, from the Cape Verde Islands—arrived each morning and as soon as the dew dried from the vines began scooping the bright red berries. At first one or two of the men balked at taking orders from a woman, but Mrs. Bumpus, toughened by necessity and past experience, soon resolved that issue, and after that everything went smoothly. The crop was bountiful that year, good news for the Bumpuses financially, but rough otherwise, in that we had to work all the harder, hauling out empties for the scoopers, carting to shore the boxes they filled and getting them to the screen house where soon another crew of women would begin culling out the rotten berries and getting the good ones ready for market. For Shirley and me the days, beginning at dawn and lasting until well after dusk, were arduous. Secretly we prayed for rain, which would have meant a day off, but fair weather held and we worked straight through until September tenth, the night of the full moon.

It was a blessing, really, the fact that we were too busy, too exhausted, to dwell on the mystery of Ronnie's ghost, if such indeed he—or it—was. After our stroll around the bog neither Shirley nor I mentioned, or even alluded to, the matter. When at last September tenth arrived we did not even go so far as to exchange glances. For all I knew Shirley might have had second thoughts and dismissed the whole thing as a figment of my imagination.

That night, dog-tired, all three of us went to bed early as usual.

"The good Lord willing, in another five or six days the berries will all be in and we can take a much deserved vacation," Mrs. Bumpus remarked, as she trimmed the wick on the parlor lamp before heading toward her room. "You two girls deserve a special treat. Maybe we can go somewheres for a day or two. Stay at a nice hotel. Go to the movies." She heaved a deep sigh. "We'll see."

"The last time I saw a motion picture show was before they invented talkies," Shirley responded with, I knew, only slight exaggeration. After scarcely more than four months of living in the woods without neighbors or electricity, I was—despite the dance in Onset and an occasional excursion into town—beginning to feel the depressing effects of isolation. Or was it thoughts of the moonlit apparition—along with the impending full moon—that really lay at the root of my feelings of bleakness and despair?

Mumbling something appropriate I lit a candle and carried it up to my room. Once there I immediately snuffed it, and fully clothed, collapsed onto the bed, with only a light coverlet to ward off the evening chill. I closed my eyes but did not try to sleep. Would Shirley remember? Would she keep her promise?

I needn't have worried. A soft rap at the door was immediately followed by her lithe figure slipping into the room. Wraith-like, she stood by the foot of the bed. Like me she still wore the outfit she'd put on after washing up before supper: a comfortable skirt and blouse. She had, however, exchanged shoes for boots.

Neither of us spoke, so as not to disturb her mother and alert her as to what we were up to. And I, for one, did not wish to break the spell—for was it not always in dead silence that the specter appeared?

I rose and repositioning the chair next to the window motioned for her to sit, but she shook her head and insisted by her gestures that I take the seat. "You know exactly where to look," she whispered—the only words spoken in the room that night.

So once again I kept vigil, while Shirley sat on the edge of the bed, like a captive awaiting rescue in some improbable romance. Despite thin clouds that smeared the face of the moon like streamers adrift in the sky, the landscape seemed even more illumined than in previous months. Objects seemed magnified beyond their daytime scope, such as the pyramids of empties that awaited the scoopers, or the wheelbarrow lying on its side, or the oak plank that served as a temporary bridge spanning the ditch between shore and bog.

And he was there, as before, having materialized the instant my mind wandered. Shirley must have sensed something, perhaps seen my body stiffen, for she sprang from the bed and was immediately at my side. I had no need to point toward the dike; her gaze was already in that direction.

Together we watched as he moved from dike to shore and along the dirt track that led to the house. When, for a handful of seconds, he disappeared into the shadows Shirley's frame trembled; she let out a sigh when he stepped forth again into the moonlight. As always, he came to a stop in the yard and tossing his head back stared up at the window. Despite the pallor, the uniform gray, that made both him and his clothing appear as if molded of wet clay, I detected a change in his countenance. His expression seemed…hopeful…if that be possible in speaking of a ghost; and I knew that the alteration must be owing to his sister's presence.

As usual he beckoned with his arm; no sooner had he done so than

Shirley broke away from the window and started for the door. I followed, hurriedly, careful to make no noise, yet desperate lest the specter (from now on I must refer to him as Ronald!) vanish before we joined him outdoors. When we reached the downstairs hallway and stood in front of the door we hesitated, but only for a moment. With a frantic cry Shirley twisted the knob, yanked the door open, and dashed outside. As I closed the door behind me I thought I heard Mrs. Bumpus call out from her room, but perhaps I was mistaken.

As we ran around the corner of the house I thought: what madness, two women in pursuit of a ghost! If ghost it be. Might it not be something worse, some evil demon bent on luring us to an unspeakable doom? Lurid, melodramatic nonsense! I can look back now and smile at such naiveté, but at the time my fears were all too real. Yet when I saw the area under my window vacant, I thought, well of course, what did I expect? But Shirley, a step ahead of me, had already spotted him—ten or twelve paces in front, retracing his route toward the dike. We spurted after him. But though he didn't seem to increase his pace he remained a constant distance ahead, turning now and then to see whether we still followed, all the while motioning us onward.

As we tore through the shadows cast by the elms a shudder wracked my frame, and I glanced longingly toward the house and the sanctuary it represented. With dismay I saw lights burning. We had wakened Mrs. Bumpus with our clamor; how would we explain to her our impetuous sally into the night?

That minor concern was immediately replaced by a greater one: where was Ronald leading us? Already he had progressed beyond the point on the dike where he customarily materialized. Exposed—vulnerable under the firmament—we were rapidly nearing the opposite shore. The wind was picking up, and with it the raft of clouds that scudded across the face of the moon. Periods of partial obscurity—during which Ronald seemed to fade—alternated with luminosity. Would we reach our destination in time? Or would the moon be occluded, and with it the spectral Ronald?

When he reached the end of the dike Ronald turned right and headed toward the reservoir. We were running now, the three of us, frantic to outpace the impending storm. The gravel roadway gave way to a rough, unevenly rutted track that skirting the reservoir led down to the river. Suddenly, at the river's edge, a dozen or so yards from the pump house, Ronald halted; instinctively Shirley and I did likewise. Panting from exertion and apprehension we clung to each other and watched as Ronald, with a final glance our way, walked over to the edge of the woods, where he knelt and groped around with his hands in the brush. Moments later he stood erect, holding a cloth sack, from which he removed a claw hammer and a small hand saw. He carried these, along with the empty sack, back to the water's edge.

With an abrupt intake of breath Shirley clutched my arm; I wondered at first at her alarm, then perceived its cause: the pump house had shifted position. Or rather, it no longer existed but had been replaced by another, shabbier structure which stood two or three yards to the left of where the original had stood. More frightening, this phantom pump house began to shimmer in the moonlight—as if viewed through water—and grow transparent. The wall nearest us peeled away, so that we stood, as it were, facing an open stage.

And on that stage a strange play was enacted.

Ronald crept into the pump house. As if in pantomime he crouched and, using the hammer, loosened the nails on the floorboard nearest the pump shaft. He lifted the grease-stained board and sawed it, though not all the way through. He loosened another floorboard and repeated the process. He then replaced the damaged boards and carefully disguised his handiwork by sweeping dirt with his hands over the cuts. When he was finished he stuffed the saw and hammer into the sack and hastened outside where he stood facing us—and stared into our eyes with his own, which were ghastly, the color, the texture, of the undersides of dead fish. Then covering his face with his hands he began to sob. His whole frame was soon wracked with sobs—sobs which, like the hammering and sawing that preceded them, our mortal ears could not hear.

The wind gusted, dense clouds brushed against the moon, and the first persistent drops of what would be a torrential downpour pinged against the leaves on the encroaching trees. In the obscurity of the storm neither Ronald nor the phantom pump house were any longer visible. Clasping Shirley's hand in mine I led her home—indifferent, the two of us, to the drenching rain, the thunderclaps, and the lightening bolts that lit the sky. We saw, from afar, the lamps burning in the house and knew that Mrs. Bumpus awaited us.

We found her sitting in the parlor, in her nightgown and robe.

"I saw him," she said quietly as we stood dripping in the doorway. "My little Ron—as he used to be. I saw you follow him onto the dike. Where…where is he now?"

We told her what we'd seen. I offered to go up to my room, so that she and her daughter might talk privately, but Mrs. Bumpus insisted that I remain there with them.

"Your father was a harsh man," she said to Shirley. "He was hard on his stepson, your half brother. Physically hard and emotionally, too. And he was rough with me. In a fit of anger he struck me once, in front of Ron. I don't know—perhaps I would have left him, eventually. But then…"

"Then there was the accident," Shirley said, and hugging her mother, wept.

≈≫

Laura placed the last of the yellowed sheets on top of the pile at her feet.

"So he lived for ten years with the guilt of what he'd done, then killed himself."

"Or," Charles said, "if you take the story at its face value, he died, or his soul, or his spirit died—figuratively at least—at the age of twelve, when he booby-trapped the pump house and caused his stepfather's gruesome death."

"It's a sad story, no matter how you interpret it," Laura said. "I see what you meant now: the grayness of ghosts."

Chomp

The head is very large and pointed. The upper and lower jaws terminate in strong crooked beaks. Owing to the low arch of the skull the eyes are placed at such an angle that the range of vision extends upward as well as to the side. The neck, which is covered with loose, warty skin, is of such length that the head cannot be completely withdrawn into the shell. The carapace has three blunt, irregular keels...The plastron is small and cruciform...The tail is long and has on its superior surface a series of blunt horny crests...

—Harold Babcock,

Turtles of the Northeastern United States

❧

The low arch of the skull...that loose, warty skin: for the first couple of sentences I thought the fellow was describing me!

A GREAT BLUE HERON STOOD POISED in the shallows at the edge of the lake: a decorative decal pasted onto the luxuriant wreaths of poison ivy crowding the shoreline.

Rick Gallagher broke the silence. "Ugly brute, isn't it?"

He said this not in reference to the heron (which he and Monteiro had for some while now been breathlessly admiring through the lens of a spotting scope stabilized upon a tripod which Gallagher, the more experienced birder of the two, had stuck deep into the turf some twenty yards from shore) but with a nod to a large snapping turtle which, disturbed from its resting place in a wallow of mud beside the trail, had begun its ponderous but inevitable trek toward the larger body of water. Or had the snapper been disturbed at all? It seemed deliberately headed in the direction of the heron, and indeed the bird, upon the too close approach of the reptile, took clumsily to the air.

Normally Gallagher, a lifelong admirer of all wild creatures, avian or otherwise, would not have disparaged the turtle. Unlike many self-styled naturalists, he did not find snappers particularly ill-favored or repulsive, nor did he begrudge them their occasional depredations against ducklings and other water fowl. In fact, as a rule he gave voice to his veneration and respect for *Chelydra serpentina*, for its toughness, its antiquity, its having survived for untold eons the vagaries of a brutal universe.

He spoke contrary to habit because he'd seen his companion blanch at the snapper, had heard his gasp of revulsion and seen him draw back (like a box turtle, Gallagher couldn't help thinking, withdrawing into its shell and closing up shop).

This wasn't the first time he'd seen Monteiro react to a snapping turtle. On one other occasion, in a swampy area in Washington County, Maine, Gallagher had seen him cringe at the sudden emergence of a snapper's head from the middle of a small pond. That minor occurrence had left Monteiro visibly shaken. He was visibly shaken now.

It was disconcerting to see a man (who, though well into his forties, was hale and of stocky build and, Gallagher knew, no physical coward) fall to pieces, as it were, at the mere sight of an admittedly formidable but essentially—if treated with due caution—innocuous creature.

Gallagher detached the scope from the tripod and tucked it into its carrying case.

"I see you're not enamored of snapping turtles," he remarked as they Indian-filed from tussock to tussock along the trail that would lead them back to dry ground and, eventually, the inn where they were staying the weekend. "You don't suffer from some sort of phobia, I trust?" He felt comfortable asking this because, although in the past they had never been particularly intimate, their mutual interest in birding had gradually, over the course of the last year or so, drawn them closer together.

They both taught at a small liberal arts college in northern New Hampshire. Gallagher had been divorced now for three years. Monteiro was a widower. His wife had been killed in an automobile accident, along with their young son, an only child, ten or twelve years previously. Neither seemed disposed to ever remarry, though Gallagher did date occasionally. Monteiro, the elder of the two, had become something of a recluse. His academic subject was American history, Gallagher's English literature.

Monteiro, who was in the lead, paused and turning slowly, said, "Phobia? You mean an irrational fear—of snapping turtles?" He shook his head. "No. Not at all. In fact I wouldn't go so far as to say I even dislike the damn things—though ..." He shrugged. "Well, I had a nasty experience, once, that involved snapping turtles. A very nasty experience. Suddenly seeing one like this calls it to mind." He hesitated, as if gauging the advisability of continuing. "Look, I'll tell you all about it this evening over a couple of drinks, if you'd care to listen."

"With the stipulation that I'm buying," Gallagher replied. "And what do you mean, 'a couple?' I've built up quite a thirst!"

⚚

"I was born in Wareham, Massachusetts, on Cape Cod," Monteiro said. "At least the folks who live in Wareham think of it as Cape Cod, though it's on the mainland (the poor man's) side of the canal. The house I grew up in was near a cranberry bog. Lots of woods, ponds, a meandering brook, and the Atlantic Ocean less than a mile from our front door. My parents couldn't afford both a house close to work *and* a summer home on the water, so they compromised, and commuted to Boston from their year-round house near the beach. That afforded me and my two sisters ample free time."

He said this rather wistfully, and Gallagher, savoring the first bitter quaff of his India pale ale, wondered whether as a child his friend might have had more free time than, if given the choice, he would have desired.

The two men were sitting in a booth across from one another, in the inn's cramped but cozy tavern.

"As you may have gathered from my name, I'm Portuguese. That is to say, half of me is Portuguese. My mother came of old Yankee stock, supposedly a direct descendent from the Mayflower, but that's never been officially established. My father's parents hailed from the Azores. They emigrated to America when he was ten. He spoke Portuguese fluently. As a consequence I picked up some of the language as a child. I mention this for a reason."

Monteiro's drink of choice was whiskey. He took it neat, in a shot glass, but sipped it slowly, one jigger for every two of Gallagher's pint draughts. The alcohol seemed to have no effect on his thinking.

"We had a neighbor, of sorts, a man named Tony Andrade who lived in a one-room shack on property attached to the cranberry bog. Well into the 1950's, I'm told, people, old men for the most part, lived alone out in the boondocks in tumble-down shanties, without electricity or running water or any of the modern amenities we take for granted. Tony's— this would have been sometime in the '60's—was one of the last of these shacks still standing.

"Tony was Cape Verdean. He'd come over to America as a young man and never really learned to speak English. He spoke Crioulo, a dialect of Portuguese. His shack stood on a clearing about a half mile from our house. An old cart road led out to it. I got friendly with Tony because, well, he was kind of lonely, and I guess I was, too, at times. And I could speak Portuguese, enough anyhow to communicate.

"At the time I speak of, Tony was in his late forties, about the age I am now. I was twelve. He'd been disabled for a number of years and lived off a combination of welfare from the town and some sort of pension. Food Stamps hadn't been invented; Tony made out quite well without them.

"He had a vegetable garden. In season he foraged in the woods for blueberries and wild grapes, and of course he had access to all the cranberries he needed. He fished off the Narrows in town and in the freshwater ponds. He snared rabbits and squirrels, and, sadly, birds. (He offered me robin stew once, but I politely declined.) He lived simply. I don't think he wanted for anything, maybe just companionship.

"Physically Tony was a wreck. He had a bad heart, brought on by obesity. Or maybe the obesity resulted from the heart condition, which prevented him from getting proper exercise. At times he had trouble breathing. Whenever he was feeling really bad I'd help him out, tilling the garden if need be, walking to the nearest store for the few items he needed. I don't wish to imply that he was an invalid. Much of the time he managed quite well. But there was that medical problem: the difficulty breathing, and the bad heart."

Monteiro signaled to the waitress for another round, and against Gallagher's protests insisted that these drinks were on him.

"This may take a while. The least I can do is pay my share."

"I'll accept payment in the form of narrative," Gallagher said. "Besides, it's not often I get the opportunity to drink all the ale I want."

Monteiro lifted his glass to his lips in a kind of salute. "The summer of the year I turned twelve was a dry one. Tony got his drinking water from a pipe driven into the ground with a hand pump attached to it. For his garden he fetched water in a bucket from the irrigation ditches on the cranberry bog. That summer, however, the ditches were often bone dry, and he had to go all the way to the bog's reservoir for his water. I remember I spent one whole morning—it was shortly after the Fourth of July—helping him lug his buckets back and forth.

"In return he was generous with his produce; he often gave me vegetables—lettuce, radishes, peas, and later tomatoes and peppers and squash—to take home to my family. I wonder if they appreciated it, though?

"Maybe it was the heat, but that July Tony's condition worsened. It became an effort for him to breathe, and once he had quite a bad spell, when he nearly passed out and I had to help him into the shade to recover. He couldn't afford medical care, naturally. There was no Medicaid in those days, just what charitable assistance the town offered. Even though I was just a kid I knew it looked bad for Tony. There were times when I was afraid I might visit his shack and find him dead.

"Most Cape Verdeans, the old-timers in particular, are devout Catholics. Tony, however, never went to church. And I often wonder, in light of what happened, if there was some influence from his past—if perhaps his mother, or maybe one of his grandparents, didn't originate on the islands but instead came from the mainland of Africa, where even today there are traditions quite different from the ones we're familiar with."

"Mumbo jumbo sort of stuff?" Gallagher asked.

"I was thinking more in terms of animism. In any case, it's only conjecture." Monteiro stared down at his glass.

"As I said, our house was situated not far from the ocean and I used to spend as much time as possible at the beach. The heat the week following Tony's fainting fit was brutal, the tides favorable; I neglected to visit Tony for three or four days running. When I finally did venture out to his shack I found him a changed man.

"I had expected to find him in bad shape. Instead, when I arrived he was busy cultivating his garden with a hoe. He'd loosened the parched earth between the rows and all around the perimeter and was about to head out to the reservoir for water. Even though sweat leaked from his brow and his clothes were drenched, his skin had lost its sickly pallor and his breathing was entirely unlabored. He grinned broadly, delighted to see me and eager to show off his new vigor.

"'Tony live forever,' he laughed, when I told him I was happy to see him looking so well. 'Come inside. I show you.'

"I followed him through the narrow doorway which, owing to his bulk, he was scarcely able to squeeze through. Heavy enough to begin with, he'd gained considerable weight since I'd last seen him.

"As if reading my thoughts he said: 'Tony eat good.' He stooped to a corner and swung open the door to the icebox. Despite the gloom (hardly any light penetrated the fly-specked panes that served as windows) I could see that the shelves were well-stocked. There were even bags of ice to keep the food fresh.

"The air inside the shack had always been stifling, fetid, putrid—owing to Tony's inability to keep the place up. But now, with his miraculously restored health, he had made a start at tidying things. The floor was swept clean, much of the clutter put away.

"As my eyes adjusted to the diminished light I noticed a jar sitting on top of the bare wooden table. Tony followed my gaze, and seizing the jar shoved it into my face for me to admire.

"Instinctively I recoiled. The jar contained water, and something else. Something that was alive. I could see it throbbing, or pulsating. But what was it? Some sort of freshwater mollusk? Some loathsome creature pulled from the muck?

"'Know what is?' Tony asked.

"I shook my head.

"Tony pounded the left side of his chest. 'Heart.'

"To my uncomprehending stare he added: 'Turtle. Big.' He said something in Portuguese which I failed to understand, then groped for the English. 'He bite with mouth.'

"'A snapping turtle?'

"Tony nodded eagerly.

"'That's the heart of a snapping turtle?'

"'Look. Still lives.' Like a proud parent showing off a newborn, Tony held the jar to the open doorway. The light that filtered through illuminated a nugget of flesh suspended in fluid like a gouged-out eye. The thing was obscene."

"I've heard they continue to beat for up to a day after being removed," Gallagher said. "Snapper hearts. They just keep pumping away. Testimony to brute, primordial forces. Another whiskey?"

"Testimony to something," Monteiro agreed. "This one lasted nearly two days. Yes, I'll have another." He waited until the drinks had been delivered before resuming his narrative.

"Tony, it turned out, had caught the snapper on dry land and cut off its head with an ax. Then he'd cooked and eaten the flesh. Somehow—here's where I think some of your 'mumbo jumbo' comes into play—he got the idea that if he preserved the still-living heart it would give his own weakened ticker renewed strength. Maybe it was something he remembered hearing from his childhood. I don't know. But evidently it worked."

"You mean he got well? In a heartbeat, as it were?"

"Call it the power of suggestion if you will. But as long as Tony kept a living, beating snapper heart in that jar he enjoyed good health."

"He went out and killed additional turtles?"

"Yes. Dozens, over the course of the summer. He lured them with the rotting flesh of their fellows. Among other things snapping turtles are carrion eaters."

"And the nasty experience you referred to earlier?"

"That took place a couple of months later. Sometime in September, shortly after school started. By then Tony had accumulated a mound of turtle shells behind his shack. He had some crazy notion of painting them and selling them to tourists. After killing the turtle and extracting the heart—and the meat, which he cooked up and ate—he'd hang the shell on a line to dry, then toss it onto the pile.

"Meanwhile the drought continued. The company that owned the cranberry bog kept drawing water to irrigate the vines, until there was hardly any water left in the reservoir, other than a shallow pool in the center. This worked to Tony's advantage, in that the snappers, along with the fish and other creatures they fed on, all concentrated into that one pool. They were easy to catch and kill."

"Must have depleted the supply," Gallagher said.

"That it did. Tony admitted he'd soon have to find another source. As it turned out, though, he had no need to. One day after school I dropped by for a visit but Tony wasn't at home. The jar stood on the table, with the latest heart still beating away, though very faintly. I figured Tony was out hunting up a replacement.

"Sure enough, when I got to the reservoir I spotted him about fifty feet from shore, knee-deep in muck. He'd just caught hold of a huge snapper by the tail and was busy hacking at its neck with an ax.

"I hollered out to him, to let him know I was there. At the sound of my voice he turned. In doing so he got careless; somehow the snapper twisted its mangled neck around and bit into Tony's arm. Startled, Tony lost his balance, dropped the snapper along with the ax, and fell flat onto his back. He floundered around like a beached whale trying to right himself. Or perhaps the apt metaphor would be a turtle on its back.

"It was comical to see him out there, mired in that wasteland of muck, too obese to regain his feet. The hot sun began to cake the slime that covered him from top to bottom. The image that came to mind was the

Tar Baby in the Uncle Remus stories. I tried not to laugh. Tony, despite his circumstances, was a proud man, and I didn't want to incur his wrath or hurt his feelings.

"I needn't have worried. For, as I stood there shaking with mirth, attempting to contain my laughter, I spotted movement along the distant shore: a snapper heading out toward the spot where Tony, cursing in Crioulo, lay flailing his limbs. It lumbered along through the cattails slowly but methodically. Then I saw another slide down the embankment and plop into the muck. Then another. Soon there were dozens, snappers of all sizes, converging into the basin of the drained reservoir, advancing like tank squadrons toward poor helpless Tony.

"It was only a matter of minutes before the first snapper reached him. Need I tell you the rest? How the mud churned bright red with gouts of blood and gore?

"They ate him, chomped him to death. He screamed, and kept screaming, until he was just a writhing mass of flesh. If he'd still had his weak heart he'd have succumbed sooner—he'd have suffered less. But his heart was strong, you know, from all those little snapper hearts he'd kept in a jar."

Gallagher said nothing, just stared into his ale.

"Later, that day or the next, I don't remember which, it was all such confusion, I went back to Tony's shack. The thing that struck me was, that all those empty turtle shells, those carapaces and plastrons, were missing." Monteiro shrugged. "Someone might have come along and taken them, I suppose. But somehow I don't think so."

Joe Baker Stops By

This story was told to me on more than one occasion, and in more than one version, back in the 1960's, when I was a student at Boston University and worked part-time for the Tweedy and Barnes Cranberry Company in Wareham. In the various renditions the names of the principals varied; I've compromised and supplied names of my own making.

"Joe Baker Stops By" won first prize in the "Strange Occurrences" contest sponsored by PRIME TIME CAPE COD *and was published in the May 2003 issue.*

ON FROST NIGHTS, during the spring and fall seasons, many of the local cranberry growers—the bog owners themselves or their trusted foremen—would gather at Sam Pearce's screen house. The ramshackle building, though set deep in the woods off a dirt road at the edge of a swamp, was more or less centrally located. It offered the men a place where they could sip coffee (or maybe something a bit stronger) and while away a portion of the long hours in front of a cozy wood stove in the company of fellow human beings.

Sometimes they stayed for only a few minutes, sometimes for an hour or two—depending on the urgency of the frost warning, and the location of the bogs for which they were responsible. The more fortunate growers had electricity at their disposal; as soon as the temperature dipped to a crucial level they had only to flip a switch and set the pumps working. Others had to deal with gasoline or bottled gas and the vagaries of engines that might, or might not, start.

All had to periodically check their thermometers, which were tucked here and there among the cranberry vines or along the dikes, near ditches and reservoirs in dark, unlighted places, far from the nearest habitation.

It was dangerous work. Muskrats undermined the dikes; it was not uncommon for a man to sink through loosened turf and twist his ankle or break a leg. A shovel or rake or other tool carelessly tossed on the ground in the light of day could in the pitch black of night lead to a fall and serious injury. Trash racks—the metal grating that trapped debris from rivers and reservoirs and prevented it from clogging pump shafts or pipelines—needed periodic cleaning. A false step could send a man plunging down a steep embankment, or into the shaft itself.

Something of the sort happened to a cranberry grower named Joe Baker back in the 1950's, they say. As Jack Perry recalled (years afterward), it was just shy of midnight one Saturday toward the end of May, when the latch to the screen house door lifted and Joe came trudging in.

"Nothing unusual in that, of course, 'cept he was dripping wet. Looked like he'd gone for a swim with all his clothes on. His boots squished as he crossed the floor, I remember that."

Sam Pearce was there: "A handful of fellows was gathered around the stove, half dozing or quietly chatting away. It was the third straight night that week we'd stayed out for frost and everybody was dog tired."

Other than a polite nod, no one said anything to Joe when he entered the room. "He wasn't the sort of fellow you joked with," Bill Harju—who was also there that night—told me. "He wasn't mean or anything. Just the kind of guy who liked to be given a wide berth. He minded his business and you minded yours. If he'd taken a tumble, why, so had we all, some time or other. Sam and me exchanged glances but didn't say nothing."

"Keep in mind the only lighting in the room was from a smelly kerosene lantern Sam kept in one corner," Jack Perry explained, when he related his version of the story. "You couldn't make out the expression on Joe's face, to tell whether he was mad with hisself or not for being so clumsy, but like I said, you could hear his boots squishing as he walked up to the stove to dry hisself off. He stood in front of the stove for a couple minutes then pulled up a chair behind it, in the shadows.

"That's about all that happened, 'cept five minutes later Bob Kelley bursts onto the scene and says, all excited, 'I just found Joe Baker dead! Found him floating in the canal to his pump house.' Bob's bog was next to Joe's, you see, and they usually stopped by one another's on frost nights.

"'Don't be a damn fool. Joe Baker is setting right there behind you,' Sam said, and we all glanced over to the corner where we'd seen him plunk hisself down, just five minutes before, but there wasn't nobody there, just a wet impression on the wooden chair, and a puddle of dirty water on the floor."

The Bogman's Tale

...a death in the family was told to the bees, and sometimes the hives

were trimmed with crepe, as if it were possible for the wandering spirit of

the dead to come back to the homestead to get a supply of honey,

if stinted of it in the last resting-place.

—William Root Bliss,

THE OLD COLONY TOWN AND THE AMBIT OF BUZZARDS BAY

❧❧

"*Even though it was late summer and the blossoms had already set, the bee hives which the company had rented for the season hadn't been removed; there were thirty of 'em, lined up in trim rows...on the clearing...*

"*As luck would have it one of the hives decided to swarm. Evidently the colony had prospered and outgrown itself. The first queen to hatch had stung the others to death, had mated with a drone, and was ready to set up housekeeping elsewhere.*

"*I was the first to spot 'em, a black smear against the sky, ragged at the edges like a miniature twister.*

"'*Look out, boys,' I shouted. 'If the queen chooses you as a likely roost the others will, too. All ten thousand of 'em.'*"

—Edward Lodi,

DEEP MEADOW BOG

OUR ANCESTORS BELIEVED IN THE SAGACITY OF BEES. The high regard in which they held these fascinating insects came about, no doubt, from centuries of observation: bees are industrious; they wander far afield in search of nectar but always find their way back to the hive; they manufacture a valuable substance, honey, and provide ahead for the lean winter months; they have a complex social system headed by a queen. The practice of "telling the bees"—of notifying the hives of any important event taking place in a household, such as a betrothal, marriage, birth, or death—is believed to be thousands of years old, dating far back into prehistory.

Informing the bees of a death in the family was held to be of particular importance. Failure to do so might cause the bees to swarm and leave the premises, with the resultant loss by the family of their precious honey (throughout the ages, before the introduction of processed sugar, mankind's only sweetener). This superstition at one time may have been relevant only to the person who actually tended to the hives; surely, if that person died and the bees were not told, they would not understand why they were not being cared for, and as a consequence would leave. Some folks carried the superstition further; they believed that when the beekeeper died, if the bees swarmed they were following his soul.

Throughout the centuries many other superstitions concerning bees have evolved. Under no circumstances must a menstruating woman touch a beehive; were she to do so, all the bees would immediately fly away, never to return. However, whenever a new swarm is placed into a hive, insert the blade of a knife under the lid, and the bees will never fly away. Should a swarm of bees settle on your property, be sure to claim them as your own; otherwise a death in the family or some other calamity is sure to occur within the year. If a bee flies through an open window into your house, rejoice; it is a sign that good fortune will soon follow. Kill a bee on the first day of May, keep it with you in your pocket or purse, and you will never be without funds.

What, the reader may be wondering, does all of this bee lore—interesting though it may be—have to do with the subject of ghosts? The answer: very little, or a great deal—depending on how you interpret the story that was told to me one summer afternoon at a craft fair where my wife and I were exhibiting our books, and which I will repeat here. The story was told to me by a man who, reluctant to be perceived by his friends and acquaintances as someone who believes in ghosts, asked to be identified only as "a Finn from Carver."

Though "Finn" is no doubt an ethnic designation, I'll henceforth refer to my interlocutor as Mr. Finn.

"I'm a bogman. A cranberry grower," Mr. Finn informed me. "As you know, bog owners keep bees around their bogs to pollinate the crops. The honey produced by the hives is only a byproduct. The real value of the bees is in helping the cranberry blossoms to set.

"Most of the growers rent hives from professional beekeepers. The beekeepers set up the hives, tend to them, move them if necessary—for which they get paid (and also get to keep all the honey). My situation, though, was a little different. My foreman—we'll call him Harry—was also a beekeeper. That is to say he dabbled in bees, more as a hobby than as a way to make money, though I paid him the going rate, and he also made a small profit from selling the honey.

"It's not everyone, of course, who's willing to work around bees. No matter how careful you try to be you're bound to get stung occasionally. Me, I'm allergic to bees and could swell up and die if I got stung. I was more than happy to have Harry on hand to care for the hives. With a regular beekeeper, the grower has to wait for service. But with Harry, if I wanted the hives moved from one location to another, I'd just have to mention it, and Harry would do it for me right away.

"You ever see a beekeeper at work?" Mr. Finn asked.

I told him I had, many a time, when I worked on the bogs. "They look like some sort of monster, or an alien from outer space, like you used to see in those old science fiction or horror flics from the fifties," I said, "got up in their baggy outfits, with protective helmets of wire mesh netting over their heads, and squirting smoke into the hives." (The hives, constructed from wood and painted white to reflect the heat in summer, from the outside resemble plain boxes; the smoke—produced from smoldering wood chips or damp hay and squirted from a device that resembles a coffee can with a long spout—is used to calm the bees into submission.)

"Half the time Harry didn't bother with the outfit," Mr. Finn said. "Said it was too much hassle. Claimed if you handled the bees properly you didn't need protective clothing." He shrugged. "For him, it worked. He didn't mind getting stung. He claimed he had built up an immunity."

At this point Mr. Finn got on with his story: "One day, it was late August, a few weeks before harvest, I was driving my pickup along a dike near the clearing where that spring Harry had placed a number of hives, stopping now and then to check on the crop, and with an eye out for muskrat damage. The bees had already done their work for the season, of course. Any day now Harry would move the hives to another location, away from the vines, so as not to pose a hazard for the workers during harvest.

"I parked the pickup on the dike a safe distance from the hives and jumped the ditch to see how the crop was ripening. I stooped over and ran my fingers through the vines, turning the berries over to check their color. When I straightened, I saw something out of the corner of my eye, a shadow maybe, moving along the shore, and then I recognized it for what it was: one of the hives had swarmed. The colony had grown too large and part of it, headed by a new queen, was leaving to establish a second colony elsewhere.

"'I'd better go find Harry,' I thought. 'He'll want to catch this swarm before it gets away.' He'd do that by following it until it landed somewhere and then nabbing the queen. Once you've got the queen the rest of the swarm follows. But hell, you know all about that," Mr. Finn said.

"But even as I looked," he went on, "I saw that there was something peculiar about this particular swarm. Now, here's where it all becomes uncertain—in my mind, that is. You can argue that what I saw I only *think* I saw—because of how things turned out. What I think I saw—no, what I *know* I saw—is this: the swarm had formed itself into a recognizable shape.

I swear to God it had taken on the shape of a hangman's noose. I didn't get that impression afterwards; I got it then and there."

He shook his head. "Maybe you can understand why I don't want my name mentioned in connection with this. People might think I'm nuts, or just making it up to call attention to myself, and in light of what happened, I wouldn't want them to think that."

He paused as if to weigh his words carefully, then plunged ahead with the story.

"You know that test psychiatrists use, where you look at an abstract drawing and interpret what you see?"

"The Rorschach test," I said.

"Right. Well, if you've ever seen bees swarm maybe you'll get my drift. Thousands of bees moving all at once, rapidly, in a writhing mass, like an abstract painting, only three-dimensional. See what I mean? It's like lying in the grass and staring at the clouds as they drift overhead. Gaze at the sky long enough and you begin to see different shapes. A giraffe, maybe, or a pirate ship, or an old man with a beard.

"So at first I thought, 'My mind is playing tricks. I just think I see a hangman's noose. Pretty soon I'll be seeing something else. Who knows, maybe a baby carriage or a French poodle.' I got into my pickup, all the while keeping an eye on the swarm, to let Harry know what direction they were heading in. I drove to the end of the dike, turned around, and headed back toward the clearing where the hives were. Harry was in the area somewhere, mowing with the tractor. Even if I lost sight of the swarm Harry would probably be able to find the bees before they settled in to their new location.

"But I tell you, I was getting the creeps. That swarm just seemed to hover there, if anything looking more than ever like a hangman's noose. As I approached, it began (still holding its shape) to move—in the direction I was headed in, toward a bay of the bog that was hidden from view by a stand of trees. That's where I thought Harry might be, and sure enough, as I rounded the bend I saw his tractor parked outside an old storage shed. Harry, though, was nowhere in sight.

"That was strange. The shed was dilapidated, at least a hundred years old, and dated back to the horse-and-buggy days when harvested berries often had to be stored for days at a time before being carted to the screen house. These days we used it mostly for storing rakes and shovels and other odd tools. Why would Harry's tractor be parked next to it?

"And why did the swarm of bees lead me to it, and then just hover nearby, in that hangman's knot?

"Can you guess what I found inside that shed when I opened the door?" Mr. Finn asked.

"I think I can," I answered. "But you tell me."

"I found Harry hanging from a rafter. He'd hanged himself. He'd always had a drinking problem, and I guess his wife had left him, and he just decided to end it all. In a panic I cut him down. But it was too late. He was dead. It's not a pretty sight, a man who's hanged himself, and I suppose you could argue that it was the shock of finding him like that that gave me the idea of the bees beforehand taking on the shape of a noose. But I know what I saw, and I know that I saw it before I ever had a notion that Harry had done himself in."

The Old House by the Bog

Sometimes now in the nights in her vitals a
cold hand felt about for the weak spot; death
could be waiting to find its way in.
Waiting for her to crack, or to lose nerve.
—*Elizabeth Bowen,*
A WORLD OF LOVE

๛

That old house by the bog…is it haunted?
Vivian, who resides there alone, thinks it is. As
for George…well, he has his own opinion.

H̲E SAT BY THE PHONE, WAITING.
Long ago he had stopped watching television. So long ago, in fact, that he no longer owned a television set. Nor did he miss it: the constant babble, the commercial interruptions, the violence and sex, the vacuity— even in the so-called "educational" shows. Now he spent the better part of his days walking in the woods, or in foul weather gazing out the window at the pond in back of the house, watching the wind ruffle the surface, the changing colors of the water as the light faded or grew brighter, the occasional water fowl that paused in its migration to take refuge there—just this past fall a mallard, and two years ago a male wood duck in full regalia.

Evenings he spent reading in the chair he now occupied: books that he had possessed for years and had read at least once before and in some instances dozens of times. Or he sat steeped in reverie—or dozing—in that same spot, in that same chair, unmindful of the passage of time.

Or, as now, waiting for the phone to ring.

❧

He had (perhaps?) been asleep for fifteen or twenty minutes when at last the anticipated call came. The abrupt *brrrr* jolted him awake. He grasped the receiver and without too much fur or fuzz managed a faint "Hello?"

"George, I—"

It was Vivian. Again. Just as he had known it would be.

Three nights in a row now.

"Vivian?"

"George, I hate to bother you. But—"

"You heard them again." It was a statement, not a question.

"And *saw* them, George. This time I both heard *and saw*."

"Vivian, I don't know what to say. I—"

"I'm frightened."

"Yes. But you know there's really nothing to be afraid of."

"How can you say that?" Her voice took on an edge of desperation. "I'm here all alone. In this house." She hesitated. "Last night when I phoned you told me I was just imagining things. Hearing things. Things that aren't here. Magnifying innocent sounds. But George. Today I *saw* them. And I am *not* imagining things."

"No. You're not. But still—"

"George, this house is haunted."

He took a deep breath. "Yes. I know."

"You know? What—"

"From what you've told me," he quickly butted in. "That is to say, I believe you."

"What am I going to do? I'm afraid to stay here alone."

He clenched the receiver. *What could he say? What could he do?*

She mistook the meaning of his silence. "I know you don't owe me anything, George. I'm the one who wanted the divorce. I know you would have stayed married to me. But I don't know who else to turn to."

"If only we'd had children," he allowed himself to say, for the first time in many years.

"Maybe things would have been different," she agreed. "Maybe—"

"Yes. But 'maybe' gets us nowhere…" He waited for her to speak. But on the other end, silence.

Suddenly he couldn't bear the situation any longer. "Look," he said impulsively, "I'll be over in a bit." Before she could respond he gently replaced the receiver on the hook.

᠅

He decided to cut through the woods on foot. He could count on a good forty-five minutes of daylight, and by taking the woodland route he would avoid the more roundabout way by car—and the subsequent driving home in the dark. It had been years since, with failing night vision, he had felt comfortable driving by night. He took along a flashlight; he'd need it for the return walk through the woods.

That is, unless he spent the night at Vivian's.

But he doubted that.

❧

The stroll along the faded ruts that had at one time—more than a century ago—marked a well-traveled wagon road between farms (which no longer existed) was peaceful, though not by any means quiet. Spring peepers kept up a loud chorus of trills and whistles as he maintained his slow, yet not plodding, gait. Birds flitted from tree to tree—spooked by his presence, or perhaps merely seeking a roost for the night.

Somewhere, far off, a dog barked.

Luckily the evening air was warm. Or so it seemed. In any case he felt no need for the light summer jacket he had, rather jauntily, tossed over his shoulder before leaving. And, surprisingly, he did not regret the walking stick he had neglected to grab from the umbrella stand. This evening for the first time in a long while he felt no lameness, no stiffness in his joints. As for requiring the stick for protection—well, ferocious beasts had not been seen in the woods of southeastern Massachusetts for some two or three centuries now.

❧

A half hour's amble through the woods brought him to the grass-covered dike that bifurcated the cranberry bog bordering Vivian's property. As he crossed the dike the house loomed into view, a late two-story Victorian which, he had to admit, certainly did fit the bill, the clichéd and shopworn description of a haunted house.

Stubbornly, Vivian had bought the house and moved there shortly after the divorce. This, despite the protests of her friends, who had urged her not to. It was too big they had argued, too secluded, for a woman living alone.

Well, in one sense her friends had been wrong. Vivian had taken up residence in the old Victorian and had stayed on, apparently happily, for some twenty years, spending her time (he'd heard) gardening and bird-watching and otherwise enjoying nature.

In another sense, though, her friends had been right.

The house was haunted.

ڡﻰ

As he climbed the slope from the bog to the driveway, at an angle that brought him to the front of the house, he noticed the "For Sale" sign. The last time he'd visited, some six or eight months ago (a dozen or so years after the divorce he and Vivian had become friends once more, though only in an amiable "for old-time's-sake" sort of way), the sign had not been there.

So. The house was up for sale.

Would the fact that it was haunted, he wondered, hurt its chances of being sold?

ڡﻰ

Shrubbery crowded the lawn—clumps of lilacs and forsythias, hollies and azaleas— and with jagged teeth darkened the flagstone walkway, biting into the encroaching twilight. With a bounce in his step that surprised him— considering the nature of his mission—George pushed the evening aside and strode up the flight of wooden steps that led to the verandah.

ڡﻰ

The new heart medicine he was taking seemed to be doing its job, with no noticeable side effects. And those daily walks through the woods were helping to keep him in shape, too. He would have thought—under the circumstances—that his heart would be pounding. Not with fright, exactly. There was no cause for fright. But with—what? Trepidation? Apprehension? Something less than dread, to be sure, but by the same token greater than mere lack of concern.

❧❧

Just as he was about to lift his hand to the brass knocker the lamp above the front door burst into light. This—the abrupt illumination—startled him more than the sudden appearance of a (fearsome?) apparition would have. Or so he thought. Even so, his heartbeat remained steady, and he swiftly regained the composure he had momentarily lost.

Obviously his presence was known. He worked the knocker anyhow, with soft, rapid taps like Morse code on a telegraph key—as if he were trying to convey a cryptic message to whoever might be listening within.

He stepped back as the door slowly opened.

Whatever it was that he had expected, it was Vivian herself who stood in the doorway. She greeted him with a rush of words, as if she had been building up to this moment for days on end. He paid scant attention to their meaning as she poured forth profuse expressions of apology for having disturbed him, and equally profuse expressions of gratitude for his having stopped by. Following her into the living room, he tossed his jacket and then the flashlight onto the sofa, but remained standing.

Vivian stood opposite him. She had on a blouse and faded jeans, as if she had just come in from gardening. Knowing her, that's probably where she'd been: pottering among the flower beds. Whenever—he remembered—during their marriage she had been unhappy or disturbed, she had sought solace outdoors fussing with plants.

He noticed—not unmindful of the irony—that spending time outside in the sun and fresh air had done nothing for her complexion. Her skin looked pale, bloodless. Her hair—gray and unkempt—strayed across her face in wispy strands.

"I suppose I must look like the Wreck of the Hesperus," she quipped, weakly, when she became aware that he was regarding her.

"Nonsense. You look fine," he lied. "Beautiful as ever."

His words brought a faint smile to her lips. "Flatterer."

So this is how it is, he thought. So unlike…so different from…whatever it was he'd anticipated.

She offered him a drink. Wisely, he declined. A drink might be pushing things too far. Best to get right down to the purpose of his visit.

He lowered himself onto the sofa, next to the jacket and flashlight. "These…ghosts…"

She sat opposite him, on an antique wooden chair: a carry-over from their marriage—a gift he'd bought her for Christmas, long ago.

"I first heard them a week ago. Only *heard* them. Didn't see them. Not that time, or the next." She leaned forward, bringing her face closer to his. "At first I thought there might be something wrong with my hearing. I kept picking up…echoes. Snatches of conversation. But no matter how hard I listened, I could never quite make out the meanings of the words."

"Is there a particular room where this happened?"

She shook her head. "Throughout the house. Or rather, from room to room. As if whoever was talking was moving from one room to the next."

"Sort of like, if a real estate agent was showing the house?"

"Why, yes. That's probably a good way of putting it."

He considered clasping her hand in his, but thought better of it, and refrained. "When you phoned you said this time you saw…something?"

She nodded. "I heard the voices again. For the fourth or fifth time. In this room, actually. I came in from the dining room, where I'd been sitting gazing out over the bog. I do that sometime. Just sit, and gaze. Anyhow, I heard the voices again. And this time I think I was on the verge of under-standing what it was they were talking about. I hurried into this room…and saw…a woman. A young woman, perhaps in her thirties. She sort of faded in and out. That is, before she faded completely." Vivian brushed away a strand of loose hair that had wandered too close to her eyes. "The strange thing is…I think she caught a glimpse of me. I don't know. She had…I guess you might call it a startled look."

"As if *she* had seen a ghost?"

"Yes. Exactly. That was my impression."

"Perhaps she did see a ghost."

He did not want to be cruel or seem heartless. But how else to proceed?

She looked at him, puzzled.

"Vivian. When I crossed your yard just now I noticed a 'For Sale' sign." He paused. "This house is for sale. It makes sense that a real estate agent would be showing it to prospective buyers."

"For sale? This house?"

"Vivian. Don't you remember?"

She stared at him, then glanced around the room as if seeking her bearings. "Remember? Putting my house up for sale?"

"Just before the holidays. You became ill. You dialed 9-1-1. The ambulance came."

"I—"

"When the ambulance arrived it was too late."

She shook her head, then brought a hand to her mouth as if to stifle a scream.

"Vivian. You died. Just before the holidays. You've been…"

"Dead?"

"For half a year now."

⁓

In the end—after a brief discourse—she accepted the enormity of what he'd just told her. Rather calmly, he thought. Of course at some level, deep within, she must have known all along…at least suspected…

That it was she—*her* spirit—who was haunting the house.

They sat facing one another. *What now?* he wondered. Would Vivian's restless spirit fully accept the knowledge he'd given her, and depart for…wherever it was she was destined to go? Or would she stay on, stubbornly refusing to leave?

"Vivian—"

"George," she cut in.

"Yes?" He'd humored her thus far. What harm could there be…

"George." She looked at him, almost sadly he thought. "Don't you see? Doesn't it make sense?"

"What…?"

"You must be dead, too."

Despite himself he burst out laughing. "Now, Vivian…"

"Think about it," she insisted. "How is it that you can see and hear me, when the others—except for that young woman for a brief moment—apparently couldn't? And George. Why aren't you afraid? You're talking to a *ghost*. You should show some signs of being at least a little bit afraid. But you're not afraid at all. George, I think you're a ghost, too."

"Nonsense."

⁓

By the time he left it was well after midnight. As he directed the beam from the flashlight onto the ground before him he thought about the long conversation he'd had with Vivian. She'd readily accepted the fact that she was dead. But she kept insisting that he was, too.

He shook his head sadly. Would her spirit continue to haunt the old house by the bog, and become a neighborhood legend? Would she soon forget all about this evening and in the future phone him repeatedly, complaining that her house was haunted?

As he entered his own house he was so preoccupied with these thoughts that at first he failed to see the body slumped in the chair by the phone. It was only when he snapped on the lights that he realized, with a jolt, that Vivian was right, after all.

Cousin Bertram's Story

*"Cousin Bertram's Story" is one of a number of ghost
stories told in front of the open hearth of a Franklin stove
one winter night quite some time ago. The circumstances
behind the occasion for these stories are themselves
interesting, and will serve as a prologue of
sorts to Cousin Bertram's chilling tale.*

Though infrequent, power outages occur now and then in southeastern Massachusetts, the result of damage to lines caused by violent storms—hurricanes or nor'easters.

Such outages are particularly inconvenient in rural areas where a temporary loss of electricity means more than just no lights, no heat, no refrigeration, no radio, television, or computer. It also means no running water, which must be obtained from artesian wells by means of electric pumps. No water for drinking, or cooking (for those with gas stoves), or bathing, or flushing. Portable generators provide a partial solution, but are noisy and cumbersome and rely on fuels such as gasoline or propane which may not be readily procurable.

During a prolonged outage families with small children or the sickly and elderly are often compelled to seek shelter in cities and towns. Others—the self-reliant, the impoverished, or those who are merely stubborn or half-witted—tough it out.

Such an outage occurred in the penultimate decade of the last century, in the aftermath of a fierce January storm which began as wind and rain but which, with rapidly dropping temperatures, ended as wind and ice, a lethal combination. The weight of the ice caused already weakened tree limbs to give way and come crashing down on exposed lines, snapping them like rubber bands—or (in the words of one of the more imaginative of the narrators of these ghostly tales) "those flimsy strands of mozzarella which adhere to the chin when one is eating pizza."

Because of its isolation deep within the woods—on a rise overlooking a cranberry bog—and the many downed lines leading to that isolation, one house in a remote corner of Rochester, Massachusetts, remained without electricity, and consequently running water, long after power was restored to most other areas in town.

The loss of power was both a curse to the house's inhibitors and a blessing of sorts. To begin with, the house was old. And peculiar.

Old, because parts of it date back to the early seventeen hundreds; and peculiar, because over the centuries a succession of owners have added rooms, ells, and sundry "improvements" to the original structure without regard to architectural design or integrity. Such haphazard additions were not uncommon in the past, when entire edifices were moved, sometimes over vast distances, and attached to other dwellings, so that a respectable gambrel might be wedded to a somewhat disreputable saltbox, or a Cape Cod to a mansard.

This particular house in Rochester, Massachusetts, was a mishmash of styles, a veritable collage, no part matching another, except by chance or the misguided whims of those subsequent owners who attempted, rather unsuccessfully, to bestow a semblance of order on the architectural chaos.

The year the storm struck there were a dozen or more occupants of the house, more or less related to one another by blood or marriage. And several house guests. And one stranded traveler (actually, a hiker in the woods who had sought shelter during the storm and who, subsequently, accepted his impromptu hosts' invitation to stay on for as long as he chose).

On the second evening of the outage several family members and their guests were gathered in the living room (one of several living rooms, though this was the largest), enjoying the warmth of a Franklin stove. Hurricane lamps and candles placed throughout the room augmented the glow cast by the cheery flames.

"We're not really snowbound. Cousin Bertram has plowed us out—all the way to the paved road with his front-end loader. But we can pretend we're snowbound," Millicent said.

She was twelve years old and had always wished to be snowbound, ever since reading, at an impressionable age, John Greenleaf Whittier's famous poem. She'd read *Snow-Bound: A Winter Idyl* at least three times. And had recognized, despite the intervening century and a half, the poet's New England childhood as being not that different from her own.

Not having electricity was almost the same as being snowbound. Besides, school would be shut down for a day or two—with luck, a whole week—and she didn't mind helping to fetch water from the ancient hand-dug well or using the drafty (though still serviceable) outhouse behind the barn, if need be. There had been power outages before during her lifetime. Though none, she thought smugly, as prolonged as this one was likely to be.

"We could tell ghost stories," she said to no one in particular as she helped pass around hot coffee and tea from a tray her aunt Elspeth, with Millicent's assistance, had prepared in the kitchen, the water having been heated on a propane-powered stove.

"That sounds like it might be fun," Elspeth said—with an emphasis on *might.* "But we wouldn't want to bore our guests." She glanced at one guest in particular: the young man seated—rather conspicuously by himself, she thought—on the upholstered love seat in the flickering shadows by the stove.

"*I* for one wouldn't be bored, I assure you," Jack Bettencourt said. He was the stranded traveler who, having lost his way in the storm, had stumbled upon the old, peculiar house just as he was beginning to wonder whether he himself might, in an hour or two, become a wandering spirit, or at the least a severely frost-bitten hiker.

He took up, in the matter of the evening's entertainment, Millicent's cause in deliberate opposition to her aunt Elspeth. He did so for the simple reason that, in the short span of forty-eight hours, he had arrived—much to his chagrin—at that stage of acquaintance with a member of the opposite sex wherein repugnance has given way—gradually, insidiously, and who knows by what perverse alchemy—to stirrings of romantic love.

Jack Bettencourt's first impression of Elspeth? That she was—well, too bossy. Especially for one so young. Scarcely twenty-two, he learned from Millicent. Fresh out of college. (Somehow she'd already assumed command of the household.) Physically, to be sure, she was a fine specimen. Petite. Cute, if you discounted her eyes, which for his taste were a wee bit too green. But what an odd, old-fashioned name. *Elspeth.* As if pronounced by a lisping child. *Elspeth.* Not his type at all.

And then, of course, he had found himself thinking of her constantly. And following her with his eyes. And becoming aware that she was following him with hers.

Damn it! If she didn't care to listen to ghost stories she could very well leave the room.

She didn't, of course: leave the room, that is. And, along with many of the others, she returned to it over the course of the next several evenings—ostensibly to listen to ghost stories.

୧୨୨

The group that found itself gathered around the Franklin stove for the final ghost story—the one that concerns us—consisted of Jack Bettencourt, Elspeth, Millicent, Sal, and Cousin Bertram. With electricity at last restored to the Old, Peculiar House, all the others had returned to their accustomed quarters and to the routines of their (to quote Thoreau) "lives of quiet desperation."

Each of the five who were present that evening had his or her own reason for not wishing to be elsewhere. Millicent's was merely a desire to prolong the fun—the illusion of being snowbound—and to put off as long as possible a return to normalcy—especially the resumption "on the morrow" (as she phrased it)—of school.

Jack Bettencourt, upon whom for quite a few days now there had been no outward restraints to leave the premises, wanted very much to spend still one more evening in the company of Elspeth—who very much wanted to spend still one more evening with him.

Cousin Bertam, if asked why *he* chose to be there, might have been hard pressed to come up with an explanation. Or at least one that he felt comfortable voicing, even to himself. As for Sal's reason for being there— well, we'll see.

୧୨୨

Elspeth and Sal had each the night before taken a turn at telling ghastly tales: in both instances rehashings of narratives they'd read in books. Because these tales were not original to the tellers, and the events reported did not actually happen, they do not fall within the scope of this chapter. However, the story that Cousin Bertram was prevailed upon to relate that last evening does, very much so.

Although the lights were "back on" as Millicent said in her Yankee vernacular, she had persuaded the others (Jack and Elspeth—seated together on the love seat—had required very little persuasion) to keep them turned down low.

"You can't properly enjoy a good ghost story in a well-lit room," she reiterated as she snapped off all the lamps except a single shaded bulb attached by a metal sconce to the furthest wall. The flickering flame from the Franklin stove provided the room's only other illumination. Although the wind had died and the temperature outside had moderated, a heavy cloud cover occluded what little moonlight might otherwise have penetrated the curtained windows.

In celebration of their last "ghost session" together, Sal had insisted on brewing a pot of coffee and whipping up a plateful of home-made pastries. After catering to the others she seated herself in the ladder-back chair previously occupied by Elspeth (but shunned by Elspeth this evening in favor of a cozy spot on the love seat next to Jack). Cousin Bertram, his sun-bronzed face buried in shadows, sat in an overstuffed chair kitty-cornered to the ladder-back.

"Bert," Sal said, "some time ago you mentioned you might be inclined to tell us something of a spooky nature that once happened to you."

"That's right, Sal. I did."

"Seems like tonight might be your last chance."

"Seems like it might," Bert concurred.

He leaned forward, so that the light from the solitary bulb reflecting off the wall fell onto his face. Though it did not fully disperse them, the soft glow lessened the shadows that obscured his features. He remained silent for several moments, sipping his coffee, then shifted his chair so that he directly faced Sal.

"This took place some twenty-odd years ago." With a nod toward Jack Bettencourt he added: "When I was about your age. Maybe a year or two younger. I had a brother then. Harold. Older than me by a year." He glanced toward Sal. "You remember him, of course, though you were only a slip of a girl."

Sal met his gaze and said: "I had a crush on Hal. I'd made up my mind that when I got a little older I'd marry him."

"I remember you took his death hard." He reached out his hand, as if to comfort her, but let it fall short of her arm.

Sal shrugged. "It was a long time ago."

Bert shook his head. "Doesn't seem so long, though. The years have a way of slipping by without a person noticing." To the others he said: "My brother was always a bit reckless. Not what you'd call wild. But the type to take chances.

"The day he died we'd gone skating on a remote area of the cranberry bogs, just the two of us. Elspeth—you, too, Milly—you'd know the place: that string of bogs, couple hundred acres all told, that stretches from behind Wilson's all the way out toward Walnut Plain. We'd chosen those particular bogs to skate on because they were free of snow.

"There'd been a hard freeze for three days running. The bogs, flooded for the winter, were frozen over—except for a few open places near some of the bigger flumes. The freeze had been followed by a couple inches of light fluffy stuff. Where the ice was sheltered the snow clung to it, but where the wind had free rein, on the more open spaces, it whipped up enough to clear the snow off the ice and allow for skating. I'm mentioning these conditions because the wind and snow enter into what happened.

"Usually when the two of us went skating, at some point we'd end up racing one another. As skaters Harold and I were about equal, that is to say pretty darn good, having spent all our winters surrounded by so much frozen water. That day was no different. We horsed around most of the afternoon until it came on toward four o'clock. We never kept score or anything like that, but as I recall in the matter of competition Harold was doing a mite bit better than me. Even so, with the sun sinking low in the sky and the two of us all tuckered out—and chilled to the bone—I was glad to call it quits for the day.

"Like I said, the snow that'd fallen the day before was light and fluffy. During the night the wind had swept it off the ice and heaped it in low drifts along the dikes. As we skated toward the clearing where we'd parked the car a violent gust skimmed the tops off the drifts and sent the snow swirling so that millions of flakes crowded the air, blotting out the sky just like a snow squall.

"The makeshift 'squall' lasted only a minute or two—but in that time something happened. It was like a veil had been draped across the sky. Maybe it was just the effects of twilight falling. Or maybe it was something else. Don't ask me what. Because even after all these years, running it through my mind time and again, I can't say for sure. What I can say is this: the wind continued to spurt in gusts, not as strong as before but strong enough to create little whirlwinds of snow—like those dust devils you see in the summer that go dancing along just above the ground. Miniature tornadoes. Sucking up leaves and debris.

"One of the whirlwinds persisted, even when the wind seemed to die down. It skipped over the surface of the bog like a ballerina pirouetting across a frozen stage. There was a shape to it that was almost human.

"The whole atmosphere felt strange. Even so I didn't pay it much mind. I was ready to plop myself onto the bank, exchange my skates for shoes, warm up the car and head for home.

"As I made a beeline for shore I noticed Harold hanging back—sort of just coasting over the ice in a loop, with his head turned toward the opposite shore. I hollered for him to hurry up—at that point I was hungry enough to eat a horse; the only thought I had was to get home to a hot supper and an even hotter fire.

"Harold kept on drifting around on his skates, like he was waiting for something to happen. I called to him again. I might as well have been hollering at the moon. He ignored my shouts—as if he'd suddenly gone deaf. He seemed totally oblivious to the fact that it was time to call it a day. Muttering to myself I turned around and skated toward him.

"So far I hadn't been paying it much mind—but about that time I noticed that whirlwind I'd seen earlier. It was still skittering around the edges of the bog. Like I said, it reminded me of a dust devil, except it consisted of snow. It had a sort of crystalline glow to it, as if the slanting rays of the sun were glinting off the individual flakes. And yet—there didn't seem to be enough wind to account for it.

"I skated up to Harold. As I approached he anchored himself on the ice with the tip of a skate but otherwise paid me no heed. That's when I realized it was the whirlwind that was holding his attention.

"'If it's all the same to you', I said, sarcastic-like, 'I'd like to get on home while there's still some chance for supper.'

"'Where'd *she* come from?' he said, in the kind of cocky tone a guy would use to his buddy at a dance, when they've just spotted a good-looking gal ogling them from across the room.

"'She who? Ain't nobody here but us rats.'

"I was annoyed with my brother, yet puzzled at the same time. He kept staring off in the direction of that damned whirlwind.

"'C'mon,' I urged. 'It's getting dark. I want to be able to see to drive home.' We were quite a distance off the paved road; there weren't any street lamps on the bogs to light the way. I didn't want to risk driving into a ditch or damaging the car on a boulder or stump.

"'C'mon!'

"Harold ignored me and kept on gawking. I was beginning to get peeved.

"'Dammit, Harold.'

"I reached out with my gloved hand to tug at his coat sleeve. But before I touched fabric he shoved off, aiming toward the snow devil—and so help me God, I'm not using the word *devil* figuratively. In the fading light the damned thing looked half-human, sort of girl-like. But I guess in Harold's eyes it *was* a girl. Because, even though his back was to me and he was too far forward for me to see his expression, I could sense that he was mesmerized by that figurine of dancing snow.

"He skated right up to it, with me not too far behind. He spoke to it—said something, I couldn't quite hear what.

"'You crazy?' I shouted.

"With Harold close on its heels the whirlwind skittered around in loose circles. It seemed to bounce over the ice in slow motion—like the bouncing ball in those old-fashioned movie cartoons you once in a while still see on TV, pointing out the words to a song printed on the screen while the audience sings along.

"Then—just as he leaned forward as though to whisper into its ear— it picked up speed and cut a quick, lopsided figure-eight, before whipping diagonally across the bog.

"With nary a moment's hesitation Harold shot after it.

"By now I was getting concerned. Reckless as he sometimes was, I'd never known my brother to act quite so crazy. It wasn't as if he was just fooling around. He knew the light was fading, and that I felt dog tired and wanted to go home. And it wasn't as though we hadn't been skating all day."

Bert glanced around the room and shook his head, still puzzled after the lapse of more than two decades. "I couldn't figure him out."

Sal got up from her seat and passed around the remaining pastries. Throughout Bert's narrative—the gist of which she'd heard before, many times over—she'd sat absolutely still, attentive to the nuances of each of his expressions, hoping perhaps that this time she could make sense of the details of the events that had led to Harold's death.

"I'm too excited to eat," Millicent declared. Even so, she plucked a fat apple turnover from the tray and began stuffing it into her mouth.

"What happened next, Cousin Bertram?" Elspeth asked.

Bert sipped his coffee, found it cold, and set the mug aside.

"Well, for a while I just stood there mentally shaking my head, so to speak. I had half a mind to just up and leave. After all, I had the keys to the car. If Harold wanted to spend the whole winter's eve chasing around on the ice, so be it.

"But of course that wasn't an option. It'd be pitch dark in twenty minutes or so. I couldn't leave my own brother stranded with the temperature somewhere down in the teens and a cold wind blowing.

"And yet—the wind *wasn't* blowing. At least not persistent. That's the part that was getting to me. I could see Harold across the ice, a hundred yards away, spinning around in circles in pursuit of a will-o'-the-wisp. A will-o'-the-wisp which I could plainly see. And which *had* to be born of the wind.

"And I tell you, I was feeling cold. Not the cold you'd expect to feel after a day out in the open on the ice. But a cold that didn't originate anywhere on this earth. A cold that entered the body and penetrated to the very soul."

Bert arched his head behind his shoulders, as if to relieve himself of a kink in his neck. He looked toward Sal. "You might be thinking I've added some of this after the fact. That I'm making it up to account to myself for how Harold died that day. But that's not the case."

"I never was clear in my head as to what exactly took place that day," Sal replied. "From my point of view it all happened so quickly. The ambulance—and so much panic and confusion."

Bert explained to the others: "Harold fell through the ice. He skated too close to the flume, on the main ditch, where the overflow prevented the ice from freezing solid. I saw it happen. I saw him drawn to the spot by that whirlwind or whatever it was—I'll call it the girl-shape for lack of a better name. Because that's what Harold saw, I'm sure of it. A beautiful young woman on skates flirting with him on the ice."

"And what did *you* see, Cousin Bertram?" Jack Bettencourt asked. "I mean, you've described it as a whirlwind made of snow. But how solid was it? Could you see through it? Did it have a fixed shape? Or did it keep shifting?" He made a self-deprecatory motion with his hand. "Forgive me for interrupting. But—having had my own encounter with the supernatural—I'm curious as to what you saw."

"I can't be any more specific than I've been," Bert said. "I saw *something*. And there's no doubt in my mind that my brother saw something similar. But in far greater detail. To the extent that he thought that what he saw was real. To the extent that he followed it onto thin ice.

"I tried to warn him, of course. I could see where he was headed and shouted for him to stay clear. But it was no use. I saw him shoot over to the flume by the main ditch, where he faltered then plunged into open water.

"I dashed over as fast as I could and skidded to the very edge where he was standing in the ditch up to his shoulders in water. There really wasn't much danger that he'd drown, because the ditch wasn't all that deep and if he could only scramble onto the dike—or even onto the vines, which were even shallower than the ditch—he'd be okay. The only danger would be if he panicked and somehow got under the ice and couldn't find his way out. That's how people drown on cranberry bogs. By getting caught under the ice, where the water may be no more than a couple of feet deep.

"Skirting the sheet of thin ice, I skated up to the dike, limped along the frozen sod to the rim of the flume, and grabbed hold of Harold by the hand. He knew what I was up to, of course, and it was a simple matter to pull him onto the dike. He was blue with the cold but seemed otherwise okay. Me, I was shaking worse than him.

"There was just enough light remaining for us to get back onto the ice, skate to the opposite shore, find the car and get the hell out of there.

"I slipped out of my parka and draped it over Harold and started the engine before changing into my shoes but even so, the heater didn't kick in until we'd nearly reached home. By then Harold's teeth were chattering like those false teeth you see for sale in joke shops. Mine, too. Were chattering. But not so much from the cold as from what I'd seen."

Bert addressed himself to Sal. "This part I've never mentioned to anyone before. I figured who'd believe me? Or even if they did, what would it prove?"

"I always felt like you were holding back," Sal said. "Like there was something about that day you wanted to tell, but couldn't—maybe because it was too awful."

"I figured at the time, it was. Too awful. Or too outlandish."

"What was it, Cousin Bertram?" Millicent—unable to contain herself—asked.

"It was that girl-shape," Bert replied. "That snow devil. When Harold fell through the ice he was in pursuit of it, like I said. He was right behind it, so as to almost be able to reach out and touch it. But the instant the ice gave way and he went into the water, the shape was gone. Like it had never been there.

"And then minutes later—when I had hold of my brother's hand and was struggling to pull him onto the dike, it appeared again. Materialized out of nowhere, so that it stood—or rather, hovered— just behind him. Peering over his shoulder. Grinning at me. Only it wasn't the visage of a beautiful girl I saw. It was a grinning skull—the face of Death.

"And then it vanished again.

"You could argue that I really didn't see it, that the face of Death was never actually there. That I was only envisioning the immediate future. But—would that be less astounding?"

"If your brother didn't drown—how did he die?" Jack Bettencourt asked.

"Heart failure," Bertram said. "I got him home. Here, to this house. We got him into dry clothes and next to a hot stove and fed him hot soup and he seemed to be fine. Joking about falling through the ice. *He* didn't remember the girl-shape, that was evident from the way he was talking. As if plunging into icy bog water washed her from his mind.

"But I couldn't get her out of mine, that was for certain. That grinning Death's face. And when, suddenly, Harold clutched his chest and keeled over, and fell insensible onto the carpet—somehow I wasn't surprised. Shocked. Horrified. But not surprised."

"I wasn't there at the time it happened," Sal remarked, to Jack and the two young women. "I'm a very distant cousin of Bert and Harold's. I lived with my parents in another part of the house—where I still live today. But of course I heard about it shortly afterwards. How Harold had died, and how the doctors said his death was due to a congenital heart condition he hadn't—nobody had—been aware of. A heart defect that would have killed him eventually, they said. The shock of the cold to his system just brought it on sooner rather than later."

To Bert she said: "What do you make of it all, Bert? Do you think Harold was lured to his death by—by whatever? Or do you think his time had come, and that other thing—the skull and all—was just a warning? Though what purpose a warning would have served—" She let the sentence trail off, as if having answered her own question.

Bert shook his head. "I don't know, Sal. I honestly don't know. I've been wracking my brains all these years but damned if any of it makes sense."

The Face in the Ditch

The town of Duxbury, Massachusetts, besides its rich colonial past,

boasts some of the oldest cranberry bogs in the country. Is it then

any wonder that one or two of them may be haunted?

MYRA FIRST SAW THE FACE IN THE DITCH the day she turned fourteen. Brian—of whom her parents disapproved—dropped by in the evening and for a birthday present gave her a six-pack of Ballantine ale he'd filched from an older cousin.

They strolled down to the cranberry bog in back of Myra's house and in defiance of a cool October breeze sat on the grassy slope overlooking the fields of sunken vines. A fat harvest moon, partly obscured by clouds, cast an eerie glow over the bog.

"It's pretty," Myra said. "And weird at the same time. Sort of like a TV left on in a darkened room."

"Yeah. With the volume turned off."

Brian plucked a can from the six-pack, loosened the tab, and handed the can to Myra.

She took a tentative swallow. "Yuk—it tastes like skunk piss. How can people drink this stuff?"

By way of answering her own question she quaffed three cans of the bitter brew. In a short while she felt tipsy and more than a bit queasy. It was her first experience with alcohol.

Brian, who in a month or two would turn sixteen, tried to take advantage of the situation by sliding his hand up her skirt. Myra tolerated a brief tug on her undergarments before slapping his face. With the world looking slightly askew and her stomach feeling not quite right, she was in no mood for hanky panky.

Even so, Brian—who had abstained from the ale, insisting that it was *her* present—made a second pass. This time for his trouble he received a sharp jab to the groin.

He cursed, and Myra told him to stay out of her life.

Embittered by the realization that while two cans of ale might have gained him entry to the portals of bliss, three only made his girlfriend sick, he stomped off, mounted his bicycle, and with a dull ache in his testicles pedaled sullenly home.

Jerk! Myra lay back against the damp sward, her knees raised and spread apart, as if inviting the moon to be her lover. Like a dirty rag a knot of clouds slid across the face of the moon and wiped it clean.

Myra shivered. How could a thing so bright look so cold?

She closed her eyes and listened to the wind sough through the grove of pines that separated the cranberry bog from the house. What if the wind had body parts, like a man? She imagined its tongue probing her ear, its fingers kneading her breasts.

If only Brian weren't such a nerd.

If only her tummy didn't feel so crappy.

A sudden urge to pee prompted her to roll onto her stomach and push herself upright. Oops. Her legs. A teensy weensy wobbly.

Shit. I can't go back to the house feeling like this.

She cast about for a suitable place to relieve herself. The pines were too close to the house. Her mom—or worse, her dad—might come looking for her and see her as she peed. Why not pee right there on the grass? She was alone. No one would see her. Only the moon, with its blind eye peering down. And the wind.

The wind. With its wispy fingers, its moist tongue, its soulful sigh as it rubbed against the boughs of the tall white pines.

She unbuttoned her jacket. Loosened her skirt.

Somewhere an owl hooted as if in derision. She ignored the owl and proceeded to undress. She took everything off. *Because I'm unsteady and might wet my clothes if I didn't.*

But wasn't deceived. The real reason, she knew, was to feel herself naked. To let the wind ruffle her hair. Caress her bare buttocks. Slither in, out, around her thighs.

She was fourteen, a woman now.

She squatted and eased the pressure from her bladder. The wind, a fickle lover, died momentarily. She ran her fingers up and down her arms and legs, feeling the goose bumps raised by the cold. Above her the universe stretched off and away into infinity.

She started to dress. Then changed her mind. Nakedness—and the numbing cold—helped her forget the churning in her stomach. She burped—a sour, bitter taste—and that helped, too.

She longed to dance but didn't dare lest dancing make her dizzy, and sick. Instead she balanced on one foot and dragged the instep of the other through the damp grass. She did this, alternating feet, until she tripped over something and went sprawling onto the sward.

Yuk. Right where she'd peed.

Gingerly she stood and checked for damage. She was okay except for minor scrapes here and there. And an odor of pee. What had she tripped over anyhow?

In the moonlight she found it: the rest of the six-pack.

Brian. What a jerk. Ballantine ale for a birthday gift!

Hey, maybe she could wash the pee off with ale.

Nah. It would only make the stink worse.

And yet—how could she slip into her clothes if she reeked of urine?

I can wash myself. With water from the cranberry bog.

She traipsed down the slope to the irrigation ditch that etched the circumference of the bog and kneeling in the thick weeds that crowded the rim aimed her butt skyward. She giggled. *Mooning the moon.* She dipped her hands into the water. It was clear, not scummy like in the summer. She cupped her hands and splashed herself, first breasts, then arms and torso, then legs.

Is ditch water cleaner than pee?

How am I supposed to dry myself?

The wind picked up, brushing the weeds against her shins, tickling her in intimate places. She thrust her arms into the air and embraced the wind, letting it dry her off. She pirouetted slowly at the bog's edge, stopping when she heard something: her own teeth chattering.

With a shudder she sobered. And felt foolish. And mistrustful. Frightened of the night.

Clouds obscured the moon. The world darkened and she became disoriented. Was the ditch to her left or right? In front or behind? She hugged herself. The wind felt so cold...

Just as she decided to open her mouth and scream the moon slipped free of the clouds and with a magic wand sprinkled a pale, powdery luminescence onto the bog. She could see again. Weeping, she clutched at the light like a blind person suddenly gifted with sight.

Tears blurred her newfound vision. So that when her gaze fell unexpectedly upon it—the face in the ditch—she thought it an illusion, a distortion, something perceived but not actually there.

But it was there. Staring. Wide-eyed. Mocking. Two-dimensional, it floated on the surface like a toy sailboat launched by children on a puddle.

She gazed at it mesmerized. A reflection. *My* reflection. She stuck out her tongue. There!

The face in the ditch grinned.

She poked her thumbs in her ears and wriggled her fingers.

The face in the ditch sank slowly to the bottom. She leaned over the rim. She could see it lying in the mud, a caricature of herself with exaggerated features: a too large mouth with too thin lips, a ski nose like an alpine slope, eyes set too close together, like a rodent's.

I'm fourteen now. A woman.

"Myra!"

"Myra!"

"Myra!"

Her parents. Calling for her.

"Myra!"

As they hugged and scolded and bundled her into her clothes and led her home she sobbed.

In the ditch the face drifted to the surface again where, rippled and distorted by the wind, it floated, waiting for the optimal time to enter her dreams.

Tortuga

To prepare terrapin for cooking, plunge into

boiling water and boil five minutes.

—THE BOSTON COOKING-SCHOOL COOK BOOK

by Fannie Merritt Farmer, 1912 edition

❧

This is the second story in the collection to feature snapping turtles,

but not the last. What is it about those reptilian scoundrels

that so tantalizes? Oddly enough, my wife declined

—she absolutely refused—*to include this*

story-cum-recipe in her first cookbook,

YOLANDA'S CRANBERRY COUNTRY RECIPES.

*P*LUNGE INTO BOILING WATER. That's the nasty part, grabbing the live—and understandably reluctant—snapping turtle by the tail and plunging it head-first into a pot of boiling water. Hard on the turtle, naturally. And by no means easy on the cook, especially when the snapper—a vile and ill-tempered creature to begin with—is the granddaddy of them all and weighs in excess of 200 pounds.

And happens to be someone you once knew personally.

Lift out of water with skimmer, and remove skin from feet and tail by rubbing with a towel.

Skimmer my ass. It's block and tackle for this baby.

&y

The snapper has ceased, at long last, its anguished writhing. (Reptilian flesh—because it's so primitive?—dies hard; this was no wham-bam-thank-you-mam five-second execution.)

So now it's time to lift the carcass from the pot (a huge black cauldron like the ones cannibals always used for boiling missionaries in those cartoons you used to see in magazines in the days before political correctness) and fetch a pair of pliers and go to work.

It's no fun being a cook, when the object you're cooking weighs in excess of 200 pounds and you've got to peel off all that tough, warty skin.

The skin of someone you once knew.

Even if you didn't particularly like him. Hated his guts, in fact.

Speaking of guts: *Empty upper shell and carefully remove and discard gall-bladder, sand-bags, and thick, heavy part of intestines. Any of the gall-bladder would give a bitter flavor to the dish. The liver, small intestines, and eggs are used with the meat.*

Bitter flavor? There's bitterness aplenty. Enough to last a lifetime and then some. As for eggs, not in this sucker.

But I get ahead of myself. First I have to *Put in a kettle, cover with boiling salted water, add two slices each of carrot and onion, and a stalk of celery.* More like a pound each of carrots, onions, and celery. And a jar of minced garlic would do no harm. I should know. I'm a culinary expert.

১৩৯

Let me explain:

We grew up together, the three of us, in a small seaside village on Cape Cod. Joey's dad owned a thirty-acre cranberry bog, on which my dad held the job of foreman. As for Rosa, her dad and her mom both worked on the bog as laborers.

Joey, Rosa, and I: the unHoly Trinity. As innocent children—blissfully ignorant of social and class distinctions—we were inseparable. We played on the beach together, rode to school together on the same bus, tromped in the woods and in the swamp together, and as teenagers, worked on the bog together.

We did everything together, except become lovers. Only Joey and Rosa did that. They dated throughout high school and eventually married—even though I loved Rosa more than Joey ever did.

Maybe if she'd married *me*...

But Joey, after all, was heir to a thirty-acre cranberry bog. And Joey, "six-feet-two with eyes of blue," was captain of the high school football team. And I had acne and hated sports and my dad worked for Joey's dad, and who could blame Rosa for loving him instead of me?

Cook until meat is tender, which may be determined by pressing feet-meat between thumb and finger.

"Love me tender," as the song goes. Like I said, I'm a culinary expert, having attended a four-year college devoted to the culinary arts. I'm a master chef. (I'm not boasting. Merely stating a fact.)

Padded out in his spiffy uniform, with his thick neck and his big fat head protruding, Joey the football hero looked a lot like a turtle peeping out from its shell, so that's how he got his nickname, Tortuga, which is Spanish for *turtle*, Rosa's parents having been born in Puerto Rico and she having learned the language as a child.

Her sobriquet for me was Ratoncito. *Mouse*, or, literally, *Little Rat*. It was supposed to be a term of endearment, but I was not insensitive to the underlying mockery. Is it my fault, if—somewhat bitter—I have lived up to the name? Little Rat.

Let me see? Shall I serve Terrapin à la Baltimore? Or Terrapin à la Maryland? Or perhaps Washington Terrapin would fit the bill. All three recipes are found on pages 175 and 176 of the 1912 edition of Fannie Merritt Farmer's *Boston Cooking-School Cook Book*.

Now, I know what you're probably thinking. You think that I'm criminally insane, that I've murdered Joey, and am cooking him up as if he were a turtle.

Not so.

If anything, I have done Joey a favor.

Let me explain.

Besides an ability to speak Spanish, Rosa acquired through her Hispanic heritage—specifically, from her *abuela*, her grandmother—certain arcane skills. Her grandmother, you see, was a *bruja*. A witch.

So you don't believe in witches? Well, I'm not going to argue the point. Time, for me, is running out. I've got more important things to do than belabor the obvious.

For example, Terrapin à la Baltimore (here, for brevity's sake, I paraphrase): *Combine three-fourths cup of White Stock with two tablespoons of red wine. Add terrapin meat, with bones cut in pieces and entrails cut in smaller pieces. Cook slowly until liquor is reduced one half. Add liver separated in pieces, eggs, butter, salt, pepper, and cayenne.*

Entrails! Yuk. Our Yankee forebears sure had strong stomachs.

As did Rosa. When we were kids, it was Rosa who waded knee-deep into dirty ditch water and captured tadpoles and salamanders with her bare hands, Rosa who made puny Miss Baker, our Fourth-Grade teacher, gag and toss her cookies by putting a live earth worm into her mouth and pretending to eat it, Rosa who cast a spell on wise-ass Billy Barnes (for making fun of her parents' fractured English) so that his face broke out with boils—ugly red sores that leaked pus and took weeks to heal and scarred him, both physically and psychically, for life.

At the time, of course, Joey and I didn't really believe, though we pretended to, that it was Rosa's spell that had caused the boils. But we learned to believe—later, when she cast spells on us, and the spells came true.

My acne, for instance. That was my reward for bursting out one day in a fit of jealous rage and calling Rosa a slut when I found out for sure that she and Joey were walking together in the woods. The acne didn't stop me from loving Rosa, but it sure as Hell made me more discreet. After that, I learned to hide my jealousy. From Rosa, and from Joey.

৵৩

So I was only a little bit surprised when, not long ago, the phone rang and it was Joey, whom I hadn't seen or spoken to in ten years.

He got right to the point: "Eddie, I need your help."

Eddie, and not *Mouse*. That was a nice touch. Joey must be in dire straits, I thought, to accord me such respect.

It was January, the slack season in the coastal town of Gloucester, Massachusetts, where I have my seafood restaurant, so I was able to leave my sous-chef in charge and immediately head down to our quaint old seaside village on the Cape.

৵৩

The cranberry bog hadn't changed much in the decade since I'd last seen it. Flooded for the season, and frozen over, its diked-off sections lay barren under the pewter skies of mid-winter like a series of vast, deserted hockey fields.

Smoke curled from the chimney of the saltbox that stood on a rise overlooking the bog, indicating that Joey had fired up the wood stove. But there was nothing cheerful about the place. Everything wore a drab gray: the smoke, the skies, the weathered shingles, the frozen bog, the bark on the bare trees in the maple swamp that ringed the reservoir behind the house.

Joey, not waiting for my knock, jerked the door open as I strode up the walkway.

I was shocked by his appearance. He seemed to have aged several decades—not merely the one—since I'd last seen him. His skin looked wrinkled, cracked, weathered, like leather left exposed to sun wind and rain.

"Thanks for coming," he mumbled as he ushered me into the living room. His voice sounded harsh, raspy, guttural, as if the words issued from somewhere deep within his chest—not at all the way I remembered it. Even though the heat from the wood stove had jacked the temperature in the room to at least eighty degrees, he was bundled in layers of sweaters and overcoats and stood shivering, as if suffering from a serious blood condition.

I couldn't keep from staring at his ears: malformed, diminished, as if rotted away by an unsightly cancer. And his nose, once perfectly straight, was hooked. Like a beak.

"*She's* doing this to me," Joey said, before I had a chance to speak.

"Rosa?"

I looked stupidly about, as if expecting her to appear from the kitchen with a tray of tea and fanciful slivers of cake.

"She's gone. Weeks ago. Took the kids and left."

"I'm sorry to hear that," I said, inanely. Not even having known that Joey and Rosa had children. "Maybe…"

He shook his head. I noticed then that he was wearing a wig. He was scarcely thirty years old, for Chrissake.

"We had an argument."

"I see. And"—recalling his vile temper— "you struck her?"

He avoided my eyes. Then nodded. "And now she's put this spell on me."

"Nonsense," I said. But without conviction. "That business about Rosa being a witch—it was just kid stuff. Have you seen a doctor?"

"Dozens. They're baffled. They want to put me in an institution. So they can experiment. To help cure me, they say. Bullshit! Only Rosa can help me. The bitch."

So that's why Joey, arch rival of old, had phoned *me*—Ratoncito. Out of desperation. Hoping I might—for old times' sake—intervene with Rosa on his behalf.

I have to confess that, even though I'd hated Joey all these years—for having won Rosa, for having played the hero while I'd played the wimp, for having helped make my adolescence miserable—I pitied him then. It was pity mixed with contempt, of course. A feeling that he in some small measure deserved what he'd got.

But even Joey didn't fully deserve the horror that was happening to him.

℞℞

With shaking, malformed hands he wrote out on a scrap of paper the address of the apartment building Rosa and the kids had moved to pending the divorce, and I drove there—after first promising to do my best to help him out.

The address he'd scrawled brought me to a quiet side street in Hyannis, with shade trees and a distant view of the ocean.

"Ratoncito!" Rosa exclaimed, more with bemusement than surprise, when she answered the door. "How good to see you after all these years. I hear that you are a successful chef."

Petite, raven-haired (with not a hint of gray), black Latinate eyes scintillating verve and vitality, she was as beautiful as ever, and I told her so.

Despite myself.

Hating myself for it

I told her so.

"You're just as beautiful as ever, Rosa. Just as I remember you."

"Ah, Ratoncito, such a flatterer. Is that why you have come here? To tell me that I am beautiful? You have heard that I have left that beast, that animal, and you hope to win me for yourself?"

"Rosa, Joey's a jerk. You should have known that years ago, before you married him. But what you're doing to him—it isn't human."

"What do you mean, what I'm doing to him? He's sick. But he won't follow the doctors' orders. Is that my fault?"

"You've put a spell…"

"Hush, you idiot, or I'll put one on you."

"So you admit it!"

"I admit nothing, *maricón*."

Stung by her insult I forgot myself. Or perhaps it was the animosity born of all the past years, all the slights, the hurts of growing up loving and losing her, that caused me to lose my temper.

"Joey's right. You're nothing but a bitch." With a parting shot in Spanish— "*Puta!*"—I slammed the door and left.

Big mistake.

ولو

I found a pay phone and informed Joey of the futile outcome of my visit. I guess he hadn't expected any better.

"Thanks anyhow for trying," he said, in that gruff, guttural voice, and hung up.

I returned to Gloucester with foreboding. Justifiably so as it turned out. The first symptom to appear was in my voice. Higher pitched than normal. Squeaky, like a rodent's. Then the fuzz on my body.

Damn Rosa!

In a panic I drove once again down to the Cape, to Joey's house by the bog. This was several months after my previous visit. Joey didn't answer my knock, and I noticed that the thirty acres of cranberry bog were still flooded for the winter, even though they should've been drained by now.

The front door was unlocked and I swung it open and stepped into the house.

It was a mess. A foul stench permeated the air. Everything—furniture, walls, carpets—stood in disarray, soiled and disfigured with claw marks—as if a large creature had lumbered about, defecating and knocking things over. The back door stood ajar.

In the mud created by the abundant April rains which Cape Cod had been experiencing I could easily trace Joey's progress from the house to the reservoir: the fresh tracks and the telltale drag marks left by the huge tail. Joey had abandoned the house for a more hospitable habitat.

I wasted no time. I ran to the barn where Joey kept the implements necessary for cultivating cranberries and found the iron-hooked pole I remembered having used as a teenager for pulling planks from the flumes along the dikes, when I worked for Joey's folks, before they retired to Florida and left the cranberry business to their son.

I waded into the shallow waters and with the hook probed the muck at the bottom of the reservoir. It didn't take long, an hour at most, to locate a two-hundred pound snapping turtle. Nor did it take long to pry it from the muck and wrestle it, with the help of a pulley and chains, to shore, turtles not being overly smart—though this *tortuga* seemed more wily than the average, and I nearly lost a pair of fingers to its powerful jaws.

The turtle reeked of stagnant water; bloated leeches clung to the soft spots of its exposed flesh—neck, tail, stubby feet. Like puny Miss Baker, I gagged and nearly tossed my cookies, then set to work scrubbing it down with a wire brush.

To paraphrase Porky Pig, that's about it, folks.

I found out the name of the restaurant where Rosa occasionally takes the kids out to dinner. With my qualifications, and the chronic shortage of help on the Cape, it wasn't hard to finagle a job as chef there.

Sure, it was tough on Joey, being boiled alive. But I figure his suffering, with that turtle brain of his, was minimal. Minor compared to what I'm in store for, if I fail to halt this metamorphosis. Even now I have to wear my chef's cap pulled low, to conceal my newly pointed ears. And the fuzz is downright embarrassing, to say nothing of my falsetto voice. And the tail.

I figure my one chance—admittedly a slim one—is to turn the tables on Rosa. By feeding her the flesh of her victim, maybe I can put a curse on her. Maybe I can then get her to reverse the one she put on me...

Yeah, I know. Idle speculation. But at least I'll have had the satisfaction of feeding her and her brats the meat of their father. Better a modicum of revenge than none at all.

And afterwards, *quien sabe?* Who knows? Maybe I can get a job at Disney World. Think of it—I won't have to wear a costume.

Oh Danny Boy

Traumatic childhood events that occurred more than a half century ago
form the basis for this story. I included an earlier, somewhat different,
version in my first book of memoirs, Deep Meadow Bog, *and a later*
version in a short fantasy novel, Witches and Widdershins. *Ask me*
if the demon is real and I will answer, yes, for he—or it—has haunted
me in memory these many decades, even if, unlike the mists from
which he arose—"a massive billowing cloud that tore itself from
the guts of the night," he wasn't real to begin with.

HALLOWEEN...

Tom Gallagher parked the car at the end of the dike and walked the rest of the way up the knoll to the clearing where Marteen's shack had once stood. Overhead, blackbirds winged southward sprinkled against the sky like grains of pepper. At the edge of the clearing Tom found a fallen log where he sat hunched against the cold and waited, and wished he were somewhere, anywhere, else.

Why did he return year after year? Why did he torture himself like this?

The late October wind picked up his thoughts, echoed the patterns of his mind in the whisper of falling leaves. *Because he's my brother.*

As the light faded and night fell the wind grew stronger. Tom listened to it moan and sob through the shadows that ringed the clearing. Or was it he himself who wept, venting the grief of twenty years?

Behind him, in the swamp, tree limbs swayed and creaked as they rubbed against one another, evoking the image of a crossroads gallows where corpses dangle from chains, rotting in the wind. A scene from some horror story Tom had once read or a movie he'd seen? Better than the actual memories he fought against but which in the end always defeated him, flooded into his mind as the mist had that other Halloween twenty years ago.

Two foolish kids and a crazy old man...

Tommy was ten, his brother Danny a year older. The shack in which Marteen lived had only one window, which faced the wooded side of the knoll away from the cranberry bog, so that as Tommy and Danny approached they had only moonlight to guide them.

They rested their bicycles against the outer wall and rapped feebly on the unlatched door before entering, Danny leading the way.

The air inside felt heavy, overheated, musty with old-man smells and the potions that Marteen brewed on the cast iron stove. An oil lamp, chimney cracked and blackened, cast a pallid glow on the bare walls and on Marteen himself as he sat on a pine rocker weaving spells in the air with gnarled fingers. His face, wizened with age and years of hard toil on the cranberry bogs, resembled a black mask topped with tufts of white cotton.

He did not look up as the boys entered but sat gazing at the far wall, at the bare slab walls, at something only he with his wizard eyes could see. Tommy and Danny stood in the doorway, waiting.

At length he beckoned Danny to him and whispered into the older boy's ear. Though he could not make out the words Tommy could hear the rich cadences of the old man's speech, heavy with the rhythms of his Cape Verdean ancestors.

Marteen spoke for a long time. When he finished Danny nodded then turned to his younger brother.

"C'mon," he said, his voice quivering with fear and excitement. "We've got work to do."

He stepped outside and Tommy followed, casting a backward glance as he slipped through the door. The flickering light of the oil lamp played tricks with his eyes. He thought he saw the old man surrounded by dim shapes, half-formed things, but when he blinked his eyes the shapes were gone and the old man sat alone staring into vacancy.

Danny tugged at Tommy's sleeve. "We've gotta hurry," he whispered.

He ran around the corner of the shack to the lean-to where Marteen stored the wood he burned in his stove. Rummaging inside the lean-to, he emerged into the moonlight clutching the ax the old man used for chopping the wood.

"You know that hawk nest we found last summer on the electric light pole down by the river pump house?"

Tommy could feel his body trembling. From the cold, he told himself. Not from fear.

"There ain't no hawks in it now," he said, eyeing the ax. "What do we need that for?"

Danny hefted the ax. "This is for after. We've gotta cut some wood. But first we've gotta climb that pole and get some hawk feathers out of that nest."

"What for?"

"C'mon. I'll explain on the way."

He dashed into the woods and Tommy ran after him. Aided by moonlight they followed an old trail that led from the knoll down to the river.

"Marteen got the idea from the irrigation system the owners installed on the cranberry bog last spring," Danny explained, threading his way through the thick brush. He held the ax in his outstretched hands as a shield against wayward briars and brambles. "He says he spent his whole life thinking of a way and now he's found it."

"Way to do what?"

"Get even," Danny replied.

As Tommy opened his mouth to speak a twig snapped back and lashed across his face. "Be careful," he complained. "Even with who? For what?"

"For what happened when he was a kid."

Danny paused, as if unable to imagine Marteen as anything other than an old man. "The island where he was born is near Africa. It hardly ever gets cold there, except sometimes in the mountains. When he was a boy a great frost came and killed the crops. The people in the village starved. His mother and father both got sick and died. Marteen almost died, too. He swore he would get even."

"Even with *who*?" Tommy asked.

They had reached the utility line that fed the pump house. The pole on which the previous year a pair of hawks had nested and reared their young was just ahead.

Danny lowered his voice. "Geada, the ice demon."

He climbed the pole while Tommy held the ax. The night had grown cold; the air was still, as if frozen into silence. When at last Danny slid down the pole he was clutching a handful of feathers. Selecting the two largest, he discarded the others.

"Here," he said. "Keep this. That way he can't hurt us."

"Who can't?" Tommy asked as he seized the feather.

Danny stuffed the remaining feather into his pocket, grabbed the ax, and started back toward the old man's shack.

"Geada," he repeated over his shoulder. "The ice demon."

Tommy gripped the feather tightly in his hand. "There's no such thing," he protested, hurrying to keep up.

"Yeah? Well, wait and see, smart ass. Marteen is gonna trick him. He's gonna catch Geada in a cage and kill him. And if he hears you talking, he might kill you, too."

Tommy kept his mouth shut after that.

They ran all the way, over the matted leaves of autumn, heedless of the thorns that tore at their clothes and the roots that seemed to stretch out with a will of their own to tug at their feet. As they ran they caught a glimpse of headlights a long way off tearing through the swamp and knew it must be the foreman getting ready to start the irrigation system that would protect the unharvested cranberries against frost.

Halfway up the knoll Danny stopped to catch his breath, then set to work cutting down maple saplings.

"We need a dozen," he said as he trimmed off the branches. After seven or eight he grew tired and let Tommy cut the rest.

Holding the ax gave Tommy courage. It hadn't been *his* idea to go traipsing off into the woods on Halloween to do the bidding of an old man everyone knew was some kind of witch. Tommy wished they'd done what they normally did on Halloween, gone out trick or treating with their buddies.

They lugged the saplings up to the shack while Marteen stood in the doorway watching. He was bone thin, and completely naked. His wrinkled skin, rubbed down with ointment, glistened in the moonlight like wet leather.

They built the cage according to his instructions, erecting it at the edge of the cranberry bog just outside the range of the nearest sprinkler head. They lashed the saplings in place with pieces of twine treated with one of the old man's special potions.

As soon as the cage was completed Marteen, voicing syllables far older than English or his native Portuguese, put a spell on it. Squeezing between two of the wooden bars he stepped inside.

"He's the bait," whispered Danny.

The moon had gone down by then; there was only starlight to see by—and the first faint hint of a dawn that was still hours away.

Marteen began to chant, slowly at first, then more rapidly, in a voice cracked and shrill. And suddenly the ground began to spurt. The foreman had thrown the switch in the pump house down by the river and the sprinkler heads were working, beginning with a low hiss like a hundred whispered sighs, growing stronger and merging into a loud hum as water from the river surged through plastic pipe and the brass nozzles spun and the water shot into the air in wide arcs, slapping the ground at the boys' feet.

It was then that Marteen sent out his challenge, shouting the words in a high voice that was scarcely human. A mist rose from the bog, a cold fog that enshrouded the cage with Marteen in it. Tommy couldn't quite see what was going on but he could hear the cage begin to shake.

And then he saw it: a massive billowing cloud that tore itself from the guts of the night, a swirl of white that loomed above the cage. He saw it solidify, crystallize into jagged shards of ice.

He saw the leering, mocking countenance, heard his brother Danny yell, "C'mon!" and saw him dash forward and hit the cage with his body while he, Tommy, stood paralyzed with fear, the hawk feather clenched tight in his fist.

He saw the cage and Marteen and his brother all go spinning down the slope into the range of the irrigation system. That had been the demented old man's plan—to trap the ice demon in the cage and melt him down with the wash of the sprinkler heads.

But something went wrong, and even as the arctic chill seized hold of Tommy and his lungs froze solid and he pitched forward unconscious, he saw the demon double and treble in size, engorged by the water and the cold that were the source of its being.

When he came to it was dawn. He was alone at the edge of the bog. The rays of the morning sun were melting the frost and the coats of ice that had formed on the cranberry vines during the night. The bog workers discovered him there a few hours later, frostbitten but alive.

They never found Danny. Or the crazy old man.

Search parties combed the swamp, dredged the river, came up with nothing, no trace of either one. But Tommy knew.

And every Halloween he returned.

This Halloween promised to be a good one. The wind died down shortly after midnight. Cold air from Canada settled over New England. Ice crystals formed on the grass and shrubs and clumps of weeds. Under a waning moon the cranberry bog shone an eerie white. The crop had been harvested early so there was no need for the growers to start the sprinkler system.

In the clearing Tom Gallagher sat and waited, letting the cold take hold of him. When he and the earth were thoroughly chilled and his joints were stiff from sitting so long he got up and limped back to his car.

The windows were coated with frost. In the last of the moonlight he examined the patterns of squiggles and whorls.

There! Etched on the windshield on the driver's side amidst a swirl of arabesques in ice: the old man's face twisted in agony, the little boy's distorted with anguish and fear.

Tom stretched out his hand and stroked his brother gently.

Oh Danny! The sun will soon be up, and in its rays you will melt away and leave me in a flood of tears.

King Philip's Ghost

Geada, the ice demon whom we met in the preceding story, is a phantasm evoked from the combined imaginations of two impressionable boys and a crazed old man. If he exists, it is only in a symbolic sense, as an elemental force of nature. The ghost of King Philip, on the other hand, has been seen skulking around southern New England on numerous occasions. Whether one of those occasions is recounted in the story that follows is up to the reader to decide.

DEEP MEADOW BOG lay in the heart of a great cedar swamp not far from the Weweantic River, and not all that far from the Atlantic Ocean. Reached only by rutted dirt tracks that snaked through the woods along forgotten Indian trails, it seemed to me, when I was a boy of twelve, the most isolated spot in the world.

Deer grazed on its dikes and hawks nested in the ancient pines that ringed its sunken fields. Every year flocks of Canada geese paused in their migration to feed in the shallows of its huge reservoir, and there was even a resident population—rare in those days—who stayed year round.

I spent my summers there, long idle days that seemed to ruffle in the wind like pages from a never-ending book.

I fished—hornpout big as cats, red perch, pickerel, fresh water bass— scoured the sand pits for arrowheads, hunted for turtles and frogs, gathered blueberries, or just lay in the grass watching the clouds roll by. Sometimes Uncle Dom, who was foreman in charge of the crew that kept Deep Meadow Bog in shape, would let me help. He might allow me to pour gasoline, or hold a board steady while he sawed it in half, or fetch tools from the tool shed, or drinking water from the hand pump on shore. He might even let me try to drive his standard shift pickup, even though my feet scarcely touched the floor boards and I wasn't quite sure how to shift from first gear to second.

One of Uncle Dom's many tasks was to keep the vines irrigated, free of weeds and safe from frost. Spring was especially cold that year and whenever the State Agricultural Station in East Wareham warned of frost on the cranberry bogs Uncle Dom would spend the night monitoring the thermometers strategically placed among the vines. If he didn't start the pump that brought water directly up from the river on time, the crop might be lost. There were sprinkler heads located all over the bog to drench the vines with a heavy spray that was moving too fast to freeze.

One night while checking a thermometer he stepped on a section of dike that had been undermined by muskrats, lost his footing, and broke his leg. Luckily clouds moved in after midnight, preventing radiational cooling—saving Deep Meadow Bog from damage by frost and Uncle Dom from frostbite.

But now that he was laid up with a broken leg, who would make the rounds at night to start the pump if the temperature dipped too low?

❧

"I know he's a grown man, but I can't send Charlie Perkins out alone," Uncle Dom was trying to explain to Grandmother. "And there's no one else to go out with him. Bill Monteiro's wife is pregnant, due any moment—he can't leave her alone. Ainu's been on a toot for the past week—lucky if he dries out by the Fourth. And Alfred is puffed up worse than a blowfish with a bad dose of poison ivy."

I held my breath as Grandmother turned to me.

"You have a report due for school, don't you?"

"Well, yeah, but it's almost finished. I can bring the books with me and work on it there."

Grandmother sighed. "Oh, all right. You're only twelve years old, but I suppose we have no other choice. Charlie Perkins is thirty, but no smarter than he was at fourteen. I just hope that two kids will be better than one."

❧

Charlie picked me up at eight.

"What's them books for?"

"School report. We're learning about King Philip."

Charlie shifted into reverse and backed out of the driveway. Uncle Dom was letting us use the pickup. Charlie's own car, a dilapidated Ford with dented fenders and scratch marks all over the hood, stood parked out front.

"I never did like ancient history," Charlie said.

"King Philip isn't all that ancient," I explained. "His real name was Metacom. He was chief of the Wampanoags. His father was Massasoit, the Indian who befriended the Pilgrims."

Charlie grunted. He was a tall, rawboned man, whose face looked leathery from being out in the weather all the time. Unlike the other men who worked under Uncle Dom—drifters mostly, or drunkards, or even fugitives from the law—Charlie was a permanent fixture at Deep Meadow Bog, able to work at just about anything to do with growing cranberries.

"You believe that stuff?"

"'Course I do. They wouldn't teach it in school if it wasn't true. King Philip's War was the bloodiest ever fought on American soil, in terms of population killed. It began right here in southeastern Massachusetts. In fact," I added dramatically, getting carried away, "a battle was fought near Deep Meadow Bog."

Charlie swung the pickup onto the dirt road that twisted through the swamp. Our headlights cut a narrow swath through the black wall of darkness. Startled, a rabbit skittered off to one side, to be swallowed by the brambles. Charlie slowed the pickup to a crawl. He leaned forward, squinting through the windshield like a tourist uncertain of the way.

"Who won?"

The words came pitched too high. Charlie was all right in daylight but as soon as the sun went down he grew skittish. He was afraid of the dark.

"The battle? The Indians. They wiped out a patrol of men sent from Taunton. Of course the Indians lost the war—they were badly outnumbered by the English. King Philip was betrayed by one of his own men. The English cut off his head and sent it to Plymouth, where it was impaled on a stake for all to see."

Charlie goosed the gas pedal, jouncing the pickup over the rutted dirt track. My head bounced against the back of the cab a couple of times before I caught my balance.

I should have known better than to talk about Indians and heads being cut off. I glanced over at Charlie. He had a tight grip on the steering wheel, so tight his knuckles glowed white in the darkened cab.

When we reached the shack that would be our headquarters for the night Charlie handed me the flashlight, then waited in the pickup while I unlocked the door.

He waited until I made sure the shack was empty before joining me.

He stood in the doorway shivering while I adjusted the wick on the oil lamp that, besides the flashlight, was our only source of illumination.

"We'd best get a fire going."

"There's no wood in the bin. Uncle Dom must have burned it all the night he broke his leg."

"They's plenty in the lean-to."

Charlie glanced over his shoulder at the black rectangle framed by the doorway. "You hold the flashlight while I carry it in." He stepped aside to let me go first.

The layer of clouds gauzing the night sky had begun to disperse.

"Full moon," I observed. "Looks like a big lemon meringue pie."

Charlie tilted his head backward. "With the crust nibbled off," he agreed. "Kinda makes me hungry."

The moonlight, though anemic, would have been sufficient to see by, but Charlie insisted on my holding the flashlight while he filled his arms with wood. We made two trips. On the second, just as Charlie, laden with kindling, stepped across the threshold a loud *whoop*! echoed from the woods. Rearing like a mechanical bear at a carnival sideshow, Charlie dropped the kindling and bolted inside. I dashed in after him.

"What was that?"

I shrugged. "Probably an owl."

"Owls go *whoo*."

"That one didn't."

Whistling—no sense both of us being scared—I gathered up the kindling and together we built a fire in the potbelly stove.

"How about some tea?" I suggested. "Grandmother packed some with the sandwiches."

The shack featured a dry sink but no running water. There was a hand pump outside. "You fetch the water while I watch the fire," Charlie said. His tone was a little too nonchalant. He avoided my eyes as he handed me the bucket.

I took the flashlight and went outside. The last traces of cloud had vanished, washing the moon clean in the star-freckled sky. The faint breeze that had promised to circulate the air had died.

Ideal conditions for a dangerous frost.

As I primed the pump from a jar left there for that purpose I thought I heard a rustling in the bushes. I paused and listened, but there was no other sound.

"Pretty soon Charlie will have *me* spooked," I muttered. Filling the bucket, I hurried back to the shack.

Charlie seemed glad to see me. "I heard that whooping sound again," he blurted out.

I poured water into the kettle. "Probably a whippoorwill."

"Whippoorwills go *whip poor will,* not *whoop!* *whoop!*"

"You sound like an Indian," I joked.

Charlie's raddled face turned pale. "That's just what it sounded like. Indians."

"Aw, c'mon Charlie! It could have been a woodcock. Or anything."

When the water boiled we made tea. I spread my books out on the floor and began to read by the oil lamp's dim glow. Charlie stretched out on the shack's only bunk.

"We'll have to make our rounds in an hour," he said. "If I fall asleep be sure to wake me."

But as I turned the pages, reading about King Philip's War and the massacres and atrocities committed by both sides, I knew he was lying awake, staring at the rough-hewn ceiling.

※

Charlie's teeth chattered as he switched on the ignition. "Temperature must be dropping."

"Frost for sure," I agreed.

We drove to the edge of Deep Meadow Bog onto the dike separating the reservoir from the first section of vines. Before the sprinkler system was installed the reservoir had been used to circulate water in the ditches on frost nights. Now it was used only in the winter, to flood the bog.

A vaporous mist rose from its surface like smoke from a smoldering fire. Skeletons of dead trees loomed like wraiths on a forgotten battlefield.

I got out of the pickup and slid down the bank to vine level. The ferns and other weeds were still slick with dew, but frost would soon follow. The musty smell of stagnant water filled my nostrils.

Directing the beam from the flashlight onto the thermometer staked at the edge of the ditch I read the mercury out loud. "Just under thirty-five."

I scrambled up the bank and into the pickup.

Charlie said: "We'd best check further down. That mist from the reservoir is most likely keeping this spot warmer."

Sure enough, the next two thermometers read thirty-three.

Charlie pulled out his pocket watch. "Ten past eleven. Bound to hit freezing before midnight. Better start the pump now."

We drove across the dike, then along shore until we came to the road leading to the river. Branches scraped against the sides of the pickup as we headed toward the clearing where the pump house squatted at the river's edge.

As we swung around the last curve our headlights lit up the slick aluminum siding. A spectral figure sprang out from the brush—leaped toward us—then vanished into nothingness.

"King Philip's ghost!" I hollered, and gripped Charlie's arm in a surge of panic.

Charlie let out a wail. He hit the brakes then slammed into reverse. Gears crunching, the pickup bucked. Then stalled.

Frantic, Charlie worked the ignition switch. Forgetting the clutch he floored the gas pedal, flooding the engine.

"Standard shift!" I yelled. "The clutch!"

Too late. Blubbering, Charlie tried to hide his head in the steering wheel, his whole body racked with fear.

"Charlie!" I shook him. "Charlie, do something. Start the truck."

He mumbled but remained inert, senseless with fright.

He was heavy but somehow I managed in desperation to pry him away from the steering wheel.

We had to get out of there. I let him slump to my side of the cab, then crawled into the driver's seat where, miraculously, I got the pickup started—and backed off the road into the woods.

As we lurched to a stop our headlights once again glanced off the aluminum siding of the pump house. And again King Philip—headless, hell-bent on revenge—shone luminous against the underbrush.

I stared, terrified. Another loud *whoop* sounded from the woods this side of the river.

I tried to tell myself it was only the mournful bark of a hunting fox, but Charlie groaned and began to shake, his arms up over his face. Slowly I opened my door to the night.

"Charlie, come on," I said. "We can't let the whole crop freeze."

He couldn't even answer me. But when he realized that I was going to leave him—I had climbed out and slammed the door on my side—he decided to go with me to the pump house.

He kept peering over his shoulder and jumping at each little sound. But we managed to reach the pump house together and I threw the switch and started the water coursing through the pipes to the bog sprinklers. We could hear the water rushing through the main pipe and I knew that now the sprinkler heads were spewing out the spray that would protect the tender vines.

Was the hero of the Wampanoags really out there, in the freezing swamp, stalking around without his head, his warriors at his side, haunting the land where they had been betrayed, where they had lost their only chance to stem the English tide?

I shivered but kept my thoughts to myself, and soon Charlie began to pretend that nothing had ever happened.

There was a killer frost that night. We rode along the dikes checking for plugged sprinkler heads and broken lines, but never saw or heard anything else.

At dawn we turned off our headlights and headed back to the pump house. Beneath the rising sun whose rays would now keep Deep Meadow Bog warm and safe everything was altered. In the light that scintillated off the newborn day only ordinary things were possible.

But half asleep, being driven home by Charlie, who was merrily whistling now, I kept trying to sort out the jumble of thoughts in my mind.

Okay, so most likely King Philip's ghost was just a trick of the light at night on the silver-sided pump house. Maybe. But before King Philip—and Charlie Perkins—I had never in my whole life been afraid of the dark.

A Gift for Halloween

Mr. Barnes lived on the edges of a swamp in a decaying house

near an abandoned cranberry bog, without benefit of electricity or

running water and with Ticklebelly—an aging, rheumatic cat—his sole

companion. In the early 1950's it was a tradition, the last day of

October, for a group of us to ride our bicycles across town

to enjoy our elderly friend's hospitality.

Mr. Barnes lived deep in the woods. Every Halloween, with our tires skidding through drifts of matted autumn leaves, and the sun sinking low in the west, we rode our bicycles down the rough dirt road that led to his house to listen to ghost stories.

It wasn't enough that he had no electricity; to add spice to our visit he neglected to light the hurricane lamp which—despite its smoldering wick and soot-blackened chimney—might have gone far to dispel the shadows that crept into the house to keep us uneasy company.

Mr. Barnes always had a pitcher of milk and a jar of cookies ready for us, and a tale or two designed to send shudders down our spines, causing us to bunch together afterwards as, homeward bound, we pedaled furiously down the dark, deserted streets of late October.

"Full moon tonight," Mr. Barnes observed, setting out the cookies he had himself baked that day in his portable Dutch oven. "Reminds me of the night I stood guard outside the pump house at Deep Meadow Bog."

"How come you had to guard a pump house?" I asked between mouthfuls of oatmeal cookie.

Mr. Barnes pulled up a rickety chair and joined us at the kitchen table. A fire blazing in the potbelly stove, and Ticklebelly, that ancient fur ball of a cat, drowsing in a corner by the wood box, lent a cozy domesticity to the scene, making the anticipation of supernatural horror all the more delectable.

"Well," he explained, "someone—vandals presumably—had set fire to that same pump house two years in a row. Both times on Halloween. The insurance company refused to insure it again. Not all the cranberries were picked—we still had a week or so of harvesting left. Without the pump we would have no way of protecting the berries against frost."

"Did you carry a gun?"

"Yep. A double barreled shotgun. On my way to the bog—I was still a young fellow then, and living with my folks—I stopped off at the foreman's. He lent me his twelve gauge.

"'Something strange is going on,' he said as he handed me a box of ammunition. 'Someone's got a vendetta against the company. Be careful.'

"As I was pulling out of the driveway a young woman ran out of the house—Sally, the foreman's daughter. I had seen her before but had always been too shy to talk to her.

"She had a small package in her hand. I stopped the truck and rolled down the window.

"'Here, take this,' she said, and thrust the package into my hand.

"'What is it?' I began to undo the knot.

"'No,' she said, laying her hand on mine. 'Later. Only if you need it.'

"I shoved the package into my pocket and tried to act nonchalant. 'So mysterious!' I joked. She was a pretty girl, with soft brown eyes, but a quirky, secretive smile, as if she knew things that other folks could only guess at.

"'Just in case,' she reiterated, and that was the only explanation I got.

I thanked her and started the truck. As I drove away I could see her in the rearview mirror, at the edge of the driveway, shivering in the cold October air.

"The pump house lay deep in the woods on the Weweantic River. I hid the truck in a pit where sand had been excavated. There was a full moon, bright enough to light the way. I left the flashlight in the tool box and took only the shotgun and shells."

Mr. Barnes paused to stare at us, one at a time.

"A fitful wind stirred the leaves that clung to the trees in scattered clusters like tattered clothing on a corpse. A skeleton had been unearthed in that sand pit a few years back. Victim of foul play it was assumed, though no one ever knew for sure. I don't mind telling you, that place gave me the creeps.

"I walked the rest of the way. The pump house sat in a clearing at the river's edge. It was brand spanking new, built to replace the one that had burned the year before.

"In the moonlight the unpainted walls shone eerily luminescent. I unlocked the door. The air inside was heavy, tainted by the stale fumes of stored gasoline (this was before they put the electric line in) and the damp that seeped up from the river. I removed an empty crate and dragged it across the clearing to a clump of maples where, sitting with my back against a tree, I had an unobstructed view of the pump house.

"I broke open the shotgun, inserted a shell in each barrel—and waited, the gun across my knees.

"To while away the time I thought of her—Sally, the foreman's daughter. I remembered her gift, the mysterious package in my pocket. I considered opening it but recalled her words: *Only if you need it.*

"The night wore on. I almost dozed off but something—a sixth sense perhaps—brought me fully alert. I strained my ears, listening, but could hear only the faint murmur of the Weweantic as it twisted through the swamp. The moon hung above the clearing like a clenched fist. I tried to relax but the feeling of unease persisted."

Mr. Barnes leaned forward, nearly upsetting the pitcher of milk.

"Then I saw it—movement at the edge of the clearing. It might have been the shadow of a cloud against the moon. But then it was there, a cloaked silhouette gliding toward the pump house. A tall figure, six foot if an inch. All decked out in some kind of robe like a depraved monk or maybe one of those KKK kooks.

"I waited to see if there were others. But the figure was alone. When it reached the pump house it stood before the door, hesitating. But only for a moment. Suddenly it raised its cloaked arm and sparks flew forth spraying the pump house like a Fourth of July rocket.

"I sprang from the crate, shouting. I was halfway across the clearing before the figure turned. 'Hold it right there!' I raised the shotgun to chest level. 'Don't move,' I warned as the figure took a step forward.

"Ignoring my words the form came toward me. A hood covered its face so that only eye slots and a slit for the mouth were distinguishable. As it moved closer a rank smell—like something from the swamps—permeated the air. I held my ground. The last thing I wanted to do was pull that trigger, but by gosh—

"'Don't make me shoot,' I shouted, as the form glided forward. 'Okay, buddy!' I pulled the trigger, deliberately aiming high, letting the pellets whiz harmlessly above the hood.

"Undaunted, the figure advanced at the same steady pace.

"Fear iced through my veins. I shrank back, half stumbling, and let the second barrel go full blast. The pellets tore into the hooded face. The cloth flapped as if slatted by a stiff breeze. An odor—the stench of something foul and rotting—assailed my nostrils. But still the—thing—came on.

"I ran. Away from the pump house, across the clearing, through the woods and onto the dirt road. I knew without having to look back that I was pursued. It was the lack of footfalls, the unholy silence—just the echoes of my own feet against the hard, flat ground—that horrified me.

"Just as I reached the truck my foot lodged against a root and, losing my balance, I fell against the fender and struck my head. Dazed, I leaned against the cold metal and for the first time glanced behind me.

"It was there, silhouetted against the trees, loping along the moonlit road like a long distance runner confident of its goal. Within seconds it would be upon me.

"Frantic, I broke open the shotgun. It would be no use against *that*, I knew. But I had to do something, anything, to stave off the horror. I groped in my pocket for a shell—and groaned, remembering that I had left the box the foreman had given me back there, among the maples.

"As I withdrew my hand my fingers brushed against the package from Sally. *If you need it.* I seemed to hear the words being whispered in my ear. Desperate, I broke the string with my teeth. Lifting the lid I emptied the contents into my palm—a single shotgun shell!

"I slammed the shell into one of the barrels just as the shadow fell upon me. Lifting the gun, I fired point blank into the mass of fetid cloth that hovered over me. A shrill cry, like the skirl of a skill saw tearing through metal, pierced the night air. And then, folding inward, the cloak collapsed, dropping to the ground in a crumpled heap.

"Shaking, I rose to my feet, bent over the remnants of what had been the cloak and nudged it with my foot. It was empty. But in the moonlight something glinted on the rotting fabric. I picked it up and, holding it against the skyline, saw that it was a silver pellet. Sally's gift."

In the hushed silence that followed, Mr. Barnes leaned across the table and, striking a match, ignited the wick in the hurricane lamp.

The sudden illumination chased the shadows from the room, but not the phantoms that lingered in our minds.

"It's getting late," Mr. Barnes observed, as we helped clear the table. "You fellows had best be heading for home. But before you go I want you to take something with you."

He disappeared into the living room. When he returned he was carrying a handful of small packets, each carefully tied with a string. He handed one to each of us.

"I don't expect you fellows will be needing these. But you never know. Here, just in case. A gift for Halloween."

Moonlight Harvest

Just how true—or if you prefer, just how factual
"Moonlight Harvest" is, I cannot honestly say. At one time
I believed that the events as related by Mr. Barnes occurred exactly
as he described them. After all, would Mr. Barnes—a hero in the
trenches of World War I, a man who had survived the Great
Depression, a man who drank only the finest rotgut
whiskey—would such a man lie?

A S A MEMENTO OF HIS YOUNGER DAYS Mr. Barnes kept on his doorstep the carapace of a huge snapping turtle.

He'd captured the turtle one day during the Great Depression while working on the cranberry bogs. After work he transported it home in the back of his pickup and plopped it into an old barrel, where he fattened it up with garbage before killing and eating it. He used the carapace—which in the eyes of us kids merited comparison with an army tank from World War I—as a doorstop. Every time we crossed the threshold we glanced down at the gruesome relic and shuddered, recalling that this was the very turtle that had caused Mr. Barnes to, in his own words, "turn cannibal."

Grasping the huge snapper by its tail, Mr. Barnes had grown careless and allowed it to take a chunk out of his arm with its powerful jaws. (He still bore the scar and would roll up his sleeve every once in awhile to remind us—and himself, he said—of his folly.) By a process of ratiocination eminently logical to the juvenile intellect, Mr. Barnes concluded that eating the meat of a turtle that had once taken a bite out of him made *him*—Mr. Barnes—a cannibal.

✎✎

Though imbued with more than his share of holiday spirit, Mr. Barnes did not decorate his property for Halloween. He saw no need for such superfluous habiliments as pumpkins carved into jack-o'-lanterns or bed sheets sewn into the shapes of ghosts. His house—situated at the end of a lonely dirt road, encased in shadows, surrounded by swampland and dense brush, with only a soot-encrusted oil lamp and the glow from a smoldering wood fire to dispel the gloom—seemed spooky enough.

To lend atmosphere to his ghost stories, Mr. Barnes had at his disposal any number of natural sound effects: the whooing of an owl, the barking of a fox, the cries of nocturnal creatures being pounced upon and devoured by predators. Add dead leaves skittering across the forest floor; the wind soughing through coniferous boughs; and branches swaying aloft, creaking against one another; and you had all the accouterments essential to a scary evening.

As we huddled around the kitchen table it was not merely what we heard, but also (and more especially) what we *didn't* hear, that contributed to the creepiness. Lacking electricity and running water—and the appliances dependent upon them—Mr. Barnes's house lacked those everyday sounds that might otherwise have given us a sense of cozy domesticity.

Unlike a refrigerator, an icebox doesn't hum, or vibrate, or jostle bottles and jars with frequent and cheerful *clinks*. Nor does a wood stove kick on, clatter and clank as if about to fall apart, then abruptly shut down—constantly calling attention to itself—the way an aging oil burner does.

Despite the crackle of flames and the occasional hiss of escaping gas, a wood stove—like an icebox—conspires to an atmosphere of absolute, and eerie, silence.

A silence conducive to the telling of ghost stories.

≈∽≈

As I grew older I never entirely stopped visiting Mr. Barnes, even when visiting him had become no longer fashionable. He was, after all, a friend.

But as the years passed by (years increasingly devoted to pursuing an education, along with the funds needed to pay for it) my visits became less frequent. Whenever I did drop by it was mainly to say hello and to ascertain that all was well. Too often I would cut my visit short with the excuse (genuine but not pardonable) that I was on my way to somewhere else.

One season of Halloween, though—when I was in my late teens or early twenties (memory is vague regarding exactly when; but it is safe to say it was some forty years ago)—I made up my mind to pay a proper visit.

༽༼ა

It was late evening, and although the date was not precisely October 31 the moon was waxing toward the full. Canada geese flocking south in jagged vees honked high overhead; smoke from burning leaves scented the air; and smashed pumpkins littered the asphalt streets, orange on black, emblem of All Hallow's Eve.

༽༼ა

That evening, seated at the kitchen table with a plateful of oatmeal cookies conveniently placed between us (they had been baked fresh that afternoon by Mr. Barnes in his Dutch oven), we chatted for a while and caught up on various topics, such as my progress at school and Mr. Barnes's progress at the art of living alone in the woods. Then, in the flickering glow of the oil lamp, with Ticklebelly curled in the corner by the wood stove, Mr. Barnes—having first lubricated his throat with a shot of rotgut whiskey—leaned back in his chair and unfolded a ghost story.

Just like in the old days.

The only difference between this time and then was, instead of an audience of many he had an audience of one.

༽༼ა

By way of preamble he cleared his (by now liberally lubricated) throat.

"Most likely you've heard the expression 'moonlight harvesters?'"

I nodded. "People who steal cranberries by scooping someone else's bog at night. The moon gives 'em just enough light to see by."

"A moon just like tonight's," Mr. Barnes said. "Full, or darn close to it."

At the end of a dead-end dirt road, with no neighbors other than the wild creatures that lived—and died—in the surrounding swamp, Mr. Barnes had no need for curtains or window shades. Moonbeams splashed freely through the upper portions of the east-facing window—and illustrated, as it were, the context of his speech.

"When I was young—maybe about your age—I worked for a cran-berry grower named…well, let's just call him 'Old Skinflint.' If I mentioned his real name you might recognize it, even though he's been dead for quite a long time. As a Latin scholar you're no doubt familiar with the expression *De mortuis nil nisi bonum*: 'Of the dead, speak nothing but good.' I'd be hard pressed to say anything good about Old Skinflint. But if I refrained from saying anything bad, why there'd be no story. So I'll compromise, and let the fellow remain anonymous.

"Old Skinflint—or 'Skinflint' for short—owned a bunch of cranberry bogs, some down the Cape, a couple here in Wareham, and one or two in Middleborough. After he died they were parceled out to his nieces and nephews, most of whom I'm happy to say are decent human beings—something Old Skinflint certainly wasn't. He earned his sobriquet by being the meanest tightwad in the county.

"Skinflint was I'd say in his mid fifties when he took me on as his right-hand man. He looked a lot older, though, with thinning white hair and a sallow complexion. And he looked gaunt—as if he didn't eat right. Tall, in excess of six feet, but giving the appearance of being much shorter. That's because he walked all stooped over, with his head bent low—as if by not looking people straight in the eye all his life he'd ruined his posture. Or maybe I'm reading too much into it. Maybe he walked that way—with his eyes cast down—in hopes of spotting loose change on the ground."

"If he was such a cheapskate," I asked, "how come you agreed to work for him? Weren't you afraid he'd cheat you?"

Mr. Barnes chuckled. "He paid me a salary, which I made damn sure I collected every Saturday.

"Hell, the most he could've gypped me out of was one week's pay—which you can rest assured, if he ever tried anything fancy, I'd have gotten out of him one way or the other. But the reason he never tried to hoodwink *me* was simple: he'd cheated so many folks over the years, nobody else in town would work for him. Without me, who'd help him out on frost nights? Who'd stay up until two a.m. gallivanting around from one bog to another checking thermometers and starting irrigation pumps?"

"And you didn't mind being in his employ?"

Mr. Barnes grunted. "'Being in his employ.' Is that a fancy way of saying, 'working for him?'"

"Well, yeah."

Mr. Barnes reached for the whiskey bottle. "Don't mind me," he apologized, and took a swig. "I'm picking on you to cover up my own feelings of guilt. Truth is, the only reason I worked for Old Skinflint was so I could be foreman—and have my own crew of greenhorns to boss around. Every year he took on a fresh batch, mostly Portuguese from the Cape Verde Islands. They'd stay for a season or two. Then, soon as they figured out they could do a hell of a lot better elsewhere, they'd move on.

"To tempt men to stay till the end of the season some of the bigger growers provided housing. Not to be outdone, Skinflint got hold of a couple of old tumble-down shacks which he moved to a clearing and joined together to form what he called a house, though it was scarcely more than a set of flimsy walls with a roof and partitions. He tossed in a half dozen second-hand bunks (some of which he'd rescued from the town dump) and drove a pipe into the ground with a hand pump for water.

"The first summer I worked for Skinflint he had me spruce up the shack for that fall's occupants. 'They'll need a new stove,' I pointed out, after I'd nailed down a half dozen loose floorboards and patched a couple of holes in the roof. 'This old potbelly has about had it.'

"Skinflint looked at me as if I'd suggested installing a marble fireplace or even a central heating system. "Taint nothing wrong with that stove.'

"'There's plenty wrong with it,' I said. 'The metal's rusted and worn so thin you could poke your fist through. It ain't safe. It's a fire hazard. It may be okay to heat water with, if they keep a constant eye on it. But for warmth on a cold night—unwatched—it could burn the place down.'

"'It's good enough for a bunch of Portagees,' was Skinflint's reply. 'If they don't like the stove I provide for 'em they can damn well bring their own.'

"'Then the least you can do is let me lay some bricks in this area, just in case the stove does overheat,' I said. 'That way—'

"Before I could say another word Skinflint let loose with some choice epithets, telling me in no uncertain terms where I could shove my bricks.

"'Mind your own business,' he finally told me, when I tried once more to reason with him.

"I got so mad I almost quit then and there. God knows I wish I had. But like I say, I was young and foolish, and swell-headed with being foreman. Even so, to spite Old Skinflint I spent the better part of the following day painting the interior of the 'house,' so it would look a little bit more welcoming to the men, a couple of whom were scarcely more than boys, who would be living for the first time in a foreign land, so far away from families and friends.

✧✦✧

"By the end of August Skinflint had persuaded five young men—fresh from the island of Brava with hardly a dozen words of English between them—to stay and work through the harvest season. He lured them by providing living quarters free of charge and by promising high wages—wages which, judging from prior experience, he would in the end avoid paying by claiming that, because of their imperfect knowledge of the language, the men had misunderstood the amount agreed upon."

Mr. Barnes paused, and cast a mournful eye at the nearly empty pint bottle which lay propped against a stack of dirty dishes next to the dry-sink. (To do him justice, I should mention that at the start of my visit the bottle had been only slightly more than a third full.)

As if to wipe away the taste of temptation he drew his sleeve across his mouth. With an effort he refrained from what was no doubt uppermost in his mind—the desire to seize the bottle and polish it off in one fell swoop.

✧✦✧

"By the end of September I got to know those fellers pretty well. Big Manny and Little Manny, Joe, Jake, and Peter. Hard workers, all of them. From what I understood of their language, I gathered that they were saving up most of their money to send back to their folks in Cape Verde.

"As to their 'home' here in the good old US of A—the shanty on the edge of the bog—I should've warned them about that defective stove. But if the truth be told I'd forgot all about it. The last two weeks of September we saw a spell of warm weather. Wood stoves was the subject furthest from my mind. Besides, I was busy harvesting cranberries. Not to mention manning the pumps for frost when the night temperatures returned to normal.

"That's my excuse, anyhow. For not doing something about that stove."

Mr. Barnes reached over, seized the pint bottle, and tossing back his head drained it dry.

"Around the last day of September the warm spell ended. On a couple of nights I had to start the irrigation pumps to prevent frost damage. Hailing from off the coast of Africa, those fellers weren't used to freezing temperatures. They kept that wood stove fired up at all times. One night—the second week in October—the shack caught fire and burned to the ground.

"When I swung by in the morning to cart the men off to work the shack was gone—reduced to just a heap of smoldering ashes. From the back of the pickup I grabbed a potato digger (which I used for clearing trash racks on the pump houses) and poked around. I found enough to show me what my nose had already hinted at: that the men hadn't escaped.

"I drove to the nearest phone and notified the police. Then I drove back to the site and waited. Once the police and fire truck arrived, I didn't hang around to watch; I drove to the bog we were harvesting that day and told Skinflint about the fire.

"He was upset. Not so much by the death of five men, but because now he had to go out and find replacements for them.

"I was still pretty much shaken up. All I could think of was those five fellers: their charred remains. Big Manny and Little Manny. Joe, Jake, and Peter. And I thought about their families back in Cape Verde.

"'The police will notify their families through the Consulate, I guess,' I said to Skinflint. 'You can probably send their pay through the Consulate, too.'

"'What pay?'

"'The money you owe them.'

"Skinflint scowled. 'I don't owe nobody nothing. If anything, *they* owe me. For burning down my building. Careless smoking, most likely.'

"'Careless smoking my eye! It was that defective stove, and you know it.'

"Well, Old Skinflint just turned and walked away, muttering. That was his way of dismissing the whole matter. I made up my mind then and there that that was the last I'd work for the old buzzard. I'd finish out the season—it would go against my grain to see perfectly good berries rot on the vines, which I knew would most likely happen if I didn't stay. But once the berries were picked, that would be it. And I'd make damn sure anyone who did go to work for him would know just what they were getting themselves into.

❧❧

"The setback caused by the deaths of those five fellers extended the harvest season into November. The bog where they died was the last to be picked.

"On the morning of October 31st I arrived shortly after dawn. As soon as I rounded the bend by the clearing where the shack had been I knew something was amiss. The pyramid of empties I'd stacked on shore the day before was gone. I jumped the shore ditch and examined the vines, which had that rumpled look they get, after harvesting, from being tugged at.

"I found vines, but no berries.

"Sometime during the night a crew of 'moonlight harvesters' had hand-scooped an entire acre. Funny thing, though—I didn't see any tire tracks from the truck that must have carted the berries away.

"Well, you can imagine Skinflint's reaction when I told him an acre's worth of his crop had been stolen. He was hopping mad.

"'Must have been a half dozen of 'em,' he mused, after he'd reported the theft to the police and calmed down a bit. 'It'd take at least that many scoopers to pick that many berries in so short a time.'

"'They had plenty of light to see by,' I said. 'Almost a full moon. And no clouds. Looks like the same for tonight.'

"'We'd best stand guard,' Skinflint said. 'With shotguns.'

જીબ્

"Skinflint lived in one of those stately old mansions on High Street built by ships' captains; he'd inherited it from his parents. He lived alone. (I'd heard a rumor that he'd been married once, but treated his wife so mean she'd left him after only a couple of months. But maybe that was just malicious gossip.)

"I swung by to pick him up after supper.

"I'd forgot it was Halloween until I saw all the kids in their costumes trick-or-treating up and down the streets. Skinflint, of course, wasn't about to waste money on candy for kids, so he'd kept all his lights off and was sitting in the dark when I arrived. I had to feel my way down the walkway and almost broke my neck when I tripped over a garden urn.

"When I rang the doorbell curtains parted and a pasty face with squinting eyes appeared in the window.

"'Dammit, it's me,' I shouted.

"He opened the door and without a word of greeting thrust a shotgun into my hands. 'It's loaded,' he said. He reached to one side and grabbed another that was leaning against the wainscoting. 'So's this one.' Joining me in the darkness, he locked the door behind him.

"I let him walk in front of me. If one of us was going to stumble and accidentally shoot the other in the back, I'd rather it was me than him."

తులు

Mr. Barnes stood up from his chair, stretched his legs, and walked over to the window where the moon shining through splashed its beams— as if from a bottomless bucket—onto the kitchen floor. He stood there for a long while, basking in the liquid light, and gazed at the sky.

"Moon just like tonight," he said, more to himself than to me.

Then, gathering his thoughts: "When we got to the bog, after driving through the woods down the long dirt road that led to it, there was a full moon hanging in the sky, just like now. It looked like a huge electric light somebody had strung there, deliberately, to illuminate the bog.

"'Plenty of moonlight to see by,' Skinflint said. 'Besides, they probably obtained extra visibility by shining the headlights from their vehicles onto the vines.'

"'Strange,' I said. 'I didn't notice any tire tracks.'

"'Well it ain't likely they carried off the boxes on their backs,' Skinflint remarked.

"'Speaking of what ain't likely,' I said, 'do you really think they'll return tonight? They must figure we'll be waiting for 'em.'

"'They might not know we're on to 'em. Or they might figure we'd figure they wouldn't come back.' He shrugged. 'I ain't taking no chances.'

"We left the pickup hidden behind a clump of maples by the pump house next to the river and walked back to the bog, where we sat on a fallen log in the shadows at the edge of the clearing where the shanty had stood. Skinflint held his shotgun cradled in his arms. I leaned mine next to me against the log but kept my fingers against the stock. We had a clear view of the bog as far as the first dike.

"It had rained since the fire; a fetor of damp charcoal tainted the air. Damp charcoal and something else. Something intangible, but close enough to the stench of death to turn my stomach and make me sick."

Mr. Barnes left the window and, grudgingly it seemed, returned to his chair.

"It was 'autumn in New England', of course, and the leaves had turned. In the moonlight the vivid colors faded and took on a sickly look, like artificial flowers left outside and washed pale by wind and rain.

"'This isn't going to work,' I said to Skinflint after we'd sat there for half an hour. 'It's too damn cold to sit here half the night, waiting for what most likely won't happen.'"

Mr. Barnes picked up an oatmeal cookie and idly crumbled it between his fingers as he glanced at me across the table. "You can see that my heart wasn't in it. Not that staying up all night bothered me any. It didn't. Hell, I was used to it, what with all the frost nights I'd already put in that season." Mr. Barnes shook his head. "What bothered me was the two of us. Me, sitting on a dead log in deep shadow, a mile or more from the nearest habitation, next to *him*—a man I despised. And each of us holding a loaded shotgun.

"After I'd spoken Skinflint gave me a look of disgust but kept quiet. Neither one of us had thought to bring along a Thermos of hot coffee. Even if we had I don't think I'd have drunk any. I could feel a hard knot in the pit of my stomach. If I'd swallowed coffee—or anything—I think I would've puked.

"The air temperature must have been somewhere in the mid thirties, but the wind made it feel even colder. I decided I'd give it another half hour then leave. If Skinflint wanted to stay, that would be his decision. I had the keys to the pickup and I meant to hold on to them.

"Now, I swear that neither one of us fell asleep. In the first place, it was too damn cold. Every once in a while I'd have to get up and stamp my feet to keep them from getting numb. And Skinflint was no different; if anything he fidgeted worse than me. And we were sitting on a rotting log; if we'd nodded off, we'd have keeled over backwards or lurched to one side and immediately wakened up. So don't ask me how a solid two hours could've passed without me realizing it. Or how the two of us could've missed seeing—*them*.

"The first thing I noticed was the moon. It had shifted position. That is to say it had climbed higher in the sky, and lit up a wide swathe directly in front of us. From where we sat we had a clear view of the bog, almost as if we were in a movie theater looking at an image on the screen.

"And then—as if a lens had been adjusted so that the image came into focus—I spotted the thieves: on the bog, on their knees hard at work, gliding the tines of their wooden scoops through the vines with a rocking motion. At first they appeared to be mere shadows. But as I stared they gradually took on a pale luminescence—as if they were being sketched in and painted by an invisible artist.

"Skinflint saw them about the same time I did. Shotgun in hand he bolted from the log and lunged forward. Without taking my eyes off the thieves I groped around for my gun, which I'd somehow let fall onto the ground. I located it by the coldness of the barrel, and grabbing it stood upright.

"But then I froze.

"It wasn't stiffness from having sat on the log for so long; it was fear—pure and unadulterated—that prevented me from moving even an inch. Anyone who hasn't seen—what I saw—can scoff. But till it happens to you, take my word. I was scared nearly witless. And *physically* unable to move.

"I give myself credit, though, for managing to open my mouth to shout a warning to Skinflint. The damn fool was plunging headlong across the clearing toward the bog and the thieves. Silhouetted against the sky, he looked like a scarecrow that had suddenly come to life, or a crazed combatant charging across some forgotten No Man's Land.

"'There's five of 'em,' I yelled. 'Don't you recognize who they are? Big Manny and Little Manny and Joe and Jake and Peter! It's *them*.'

"But he didn't hear me. Or wasn't listening. Or didn't give a hoot.

"'I'll fix 'em!' he shouted and began blasting away with both barrels.

"Unfazed, the five men—I won't call them thieves; they were after all only taking what was owed to them—the five men went on with their work, as if Skinflint was just an amused spectator, or a casual passerby, and not a madman intent on blasting them away with a shotgun.

"And he was a madman, I swear. I think at some point there came upon him the realization of what they were, and of what *he* was, and what he had done and not done. And it caused him to snap.

"As he raced across the clearing toward the bog he kept stopping to reload and fire, even though the blasts were having no effect whatsoever. But when he came to the ditch he didn't even pause but kept on running and stumbled headlong into it. And—it appears, from the autopsy the coroner later performed on his body—broke his neck.

"Fell and broke his neck. That's what the coroner's report said. But that's not how I saw it.

"How I saw it was, he cleared the ditch and ran right up to Big Manny, and it was Big Manny who left off scooping berries long enough to seize hold of Skinflint by the throat and twist his neck around until it snapped. Then he flung the body into the ditch, like it was a piece of trash, and resumed scooping.

ళ్ళు

"In those days, you see," Mr. Barnes said a bit later, after he'd poured himself a swig from a freshly opened bottle, "even as now, there were unscrupulous growers who were willing to accept stolen cranberries and sell them as their own and spilt the profits with the thieves. Don't ask me how they managed it, but I'm convinced that those five fellers—the *ghosts* of those five fellers—harvested the berries from that bog in order to get the money Skinflint owned them (as well as the money that, by dying, they would not be earning in years to come) in order to send it back home to their folks in Cape Verde.

ళ్ళు

"I hightailed it out of there, of course, and concocted a story to explain to the police what had happened. At first they thought I was pulling a Halloween prank, or that I was drunk—I guess I wasn't acting all that rational, after what I'd seen—but I finally convinced them that they'd better go and check up on Old Skinflint. And like I said, they found him in the ditch, with his neck broken.

"Funny thing, though—the next morning another acre of crop was missing.

"And I'll tell you something else. Scared as I was, the next night I went back, and waited—this time in the pickup with the motor running and the heater on—and sure enough they showed up again. Only this time there were six of them.

"Big Manny and Little Manny, and Joe and Jake and Peter. And Skinflint, on his knees, scooping away along side of them.

"And I'll tell you another thing. Skinflint looked different from the others. The other five shone sort of pale, like congealed moonlight. But

Skinflint seemed to glow, sort of red and yellow, as if with a flickering flame. As if he was fighting an internal fire and could keep himself from burning up only by pitching in and scooping like a madman.

"I didn't go back after that. But I heard, as the years passed, that those acres never would produce berries again. The nephew who inherited that particular bog finally gave up and sold it for house lots."

Murder on the Bogs

Search for the town of Bayard on your map of Cape Cod,

and chances are you won't find it.

You will however (if you dare to visit the Cape after reading this story)

find several towns more or less similar to Bayard—despite rampant

development, still somewhat rural. With cranberry bogs,

a town beach, and a lonely stretch of barren, wind-swept

dunes. A small police force consisting of a chief and a

handful of officers. A Board of Selectmen. And the

usual complement of thieves, murderers, and

psychopaths.

I F HELL HAS A GOOD SIDE I HAVEN'T SEEN IT. But I have seen the bad side of Hell—or at least the bad side of human nature. And the good side, too. And if what I've just said doesn't make a whole lot of sense...

Do you remember reading about the child on Cape Cod who went missing last summer? His name was Bobby Santos. Twelve years old and missing for five days. Even though there was no evidence of foul play, no strange men seen talking to Bobby, no suspicious cars cruising the street where he lived, the police had seen fit to question me. Twice.

Last Thursday had I noticed Bobby playing in the woods behind his house? Had I ever spoken to the boy? Why, exactly, had I chosen to stroll into the swamp behind the reservoir during my lunch break? Had I ever been arrested?

It was the Police Chief himself, Spoke Coffin, who asked the questions, while standing ankle-deep in cranberry vines and swatting brown-tail flies with his sweat-stained Smokey-the-Bear chapeau.

Did I, you may wonder, rate a ranking investigator the likes of Spoke Coffin because of my importance as a suspect?

Naw. The resources of the Town of Bayard are few, the police chief's duties many and varied: directing traffic, patrolling the beaches, handing out tickets for parking violations, questioning the occasional murder suspect. More often than not you can find Spoke swilling coffee and swapping gossip with the locals at Maude's Home Eatery out on the point.

Spoke, one of those same locals informed me, earned his moniker not because of any oratorical skills but because of his uncanny resemblance to the spoke of a wagon wheel. A rawboned galoot in his mid to late thirties with a carpet of straw under his Smokey-the-Bear and an Adam's apple big as a goiter.

Hey, I'm not maligning the guy. He was only a small town cop doing his job. Heck, I *liked* being questioned. Preferred it to swinging a scythe, which is what I'd been doing both times Spoke arrived on the scene in his role of Grand Inquisitor.

"I'm working my way through college," I explained for the tenth—or maybe the twentieth—time. I slid the whetstone from my hip pocket and leaning against the handle of the upright scythe sharpened the blade with the brisk, steady strokes an experienced bog worker had taught me. "The money from this summer job will pay for another semester at Boston University. I'm majoring in English. I'm a poet. You haven't heard of me because I haven't published anything. Yet."

I gripped the handle of the scythe like Old Father Time. Or should that be the Grim Reaper?

Suddenly I saw the blade gliding like a scimitar through Spoke's shirt into his soft belly, gutting him like a flounder. All in my mind, of course. Not something I'd actually do—just an image I might someday use in a poem.

So on Monday afternoon when for the third time I spotted Spoke's cruiser tearing across the dike I figured, oops! Most likely the kid's turned up dead and they're going to try to pin the blame on me. On purely circumstantial evidence, of course—I'm a stranger in town, the house I room at is diagonally across the street from Bobby's, and the cranberry bog I spend my days at is a short hike through the woods to his back yard. Add the fact, emphasized by Spoke in his interrogations, that I don't have a girlfriend (and therefore must be some kind of pervert), and the Commonwealth of Massachusetts rests its case, Your Honor.

Instead of pulling up to where I stood lopping off the heads of errant weeds, the Chief of Bayard's finest surprised me by halting next to the flume which connects the reservoir to the bog. With scarcely a glance at *moi* he swung open his door and dangled his feet over the turf to stare at the sepia-toned water as if plumbing its depths for clues.

He made me nervous. What was his game? Some bumpkin ploy to make me crack? *Talk, or I'll park on this dike all day, by golly.*

The sun cut like an acetylene torch through the ozone-depleted stratosphere. Humid air hung over the bog like a noxious gas: the muggy, in-your-face weather that browntails thrive on. Whets their appetite. When the temperature hits the nineties they go berserk, attack with kamikaze abandon.

Images of a crucified Spoke dominated my thoughts. I could see him lashed naked to the top of the cruiser, swarms of voracious browntails feasting on his sunburned flesh. Death of a Thousand Bites.

Aw, basically I'm a good Joe and wouldn't torture anyone. Not unless they deserved it. Poor Spoke. He was only doing his job.

A Dodge Stealth appeared and like a sleek beetle creeping over a log slowly traversed the dike. If my eyes bulged, could I help it? As the Stealth rolled to a stop just short of Spoke's cruiser a young woman climbed out. She had on shorts and some sort of flimsy top—gazing at curves like hers you don't pay much heed to clothing. Don't get me wrong; I'm not the lascivious type. But the sight of those gams sent the sap surging, let me tell you.

Spoke and the woman stood chatting for awhile, Spoke's Adam's apple working overtime. Once or twice they glanced my way. Swishing the scythe over the stubs of weeds I'd beheaded hours earlier, I edged closer.

Spoke climbed into his blue-and-white. Aiming herself in my direction, the object of my scrutiny slid down the grassy slope and jumped the shore ditch onto the vines.

"I'm Brenda Rawlings. You work for my Gramps."

Setting the scythe aside I grasped her proffered hand. It felt soft as a velvet glove, and cool, as if bathed in perfumed water. I held boorishly on until she gently slipped it free.

"Chet Sullivan," I mumbled.

"That boy that's missing—Chief Coffin thinks his body may be somewhere in the reservoir." As she spoke her eyes shifted hue, from a dark aqua to soft violet. Like shadows on pavement when the light thickens just before dusk. Amethyst eyes.

"He thinks I may have killed him," I blurted out.

"He mentioned having questioned you." She smiled at my awkwardness. "It's routine, I'm sure." Shrugging, she added: "It's wicked hot. You must need a break; come sit with us on the dike. Don't worry about Gramps. He's on vacation in Canada and left me in charge."

We sat in shade created by the Stealth and drank orange soda from a cooler packed with ice. Idyllic, with only an occasional browntail to mar the beatitude.

"We're waiting for the Corpse Finder."

"The who?"

Laughing, she leaned closer and whispered: "Chief Coffin hired some character who lives in the swamp and claims to be able to locate bodies."

I looked at the skeletal remains of trees rising from the reservoir like gothic tombstones. "Who could ever find a body in there? Too shallow for divers. You couldn't dredge it, not with all those stumps and roots. You'd have to drain it."

As we chatted a faded red pickup pulled up behind the Stealth. A young woman—she didn't look much older than sixteen—slid from the cab and without a word of greeting hopped onto the back, next to an aluminum skiff, and began fossicking through an assortment of boxes and crates.

Spoke approached and leaned against the sideboard. "Where's Toot?"

"Sick with the gout." She continued her search without looking up. She had on dungaree cutoffs, frizzy at the ends, and a man's shortsleeved shirt tucked under the waistband. Despite the tomboyish effect I found her attractive. She had a healthy, dark complexion—part Wampanoag, I later learned.

"He sent you instead?"

"Uh huh." She poked around until she found a thick coil of nylon cord. Heedless of whoever might be standing in the way she flung the coil blindly over the sideboard.

"You'd be Pearl Starbuck, Toot's daughter." Spoke nodded toward the reservoir. "You gonna be able to find that boy if he's in there?"

"I ain't. It might." She pointed toward a crate wedged next to the skiff's bow.

Spoke cocked a dubious eye. "If that's a dog you got in there you're wasting my time."

Pearl unlatched the crate. "Stick your head in there and see if it's a dog."

Brenda snickered. Scowling, Spoke kept silent as Pearl thrust her hand into the crate and dragged out a snapping turtle, which she held on to by the tail. Hissing like a fiend from Hell the reptile clawed at the air; twisting its neck it strained to bring its powerful jaws within snapping range of Pearl's flesh.

Gripping my forearm, Brenda dug her fingers deep into my skin.

From tail to snout the turtle measured thirty-six inches or more. Holding it at arm's length like a severed head, Pearl pivoted to the side of the truck where Spoke stood.

"You take him while I untie the boat."

Spoke yanked his head back just in time to save his Adam's apple. "Keep that thing away from me! You're supposed to locate the Santos boy's body, not mutilate mine."

Pearl turned toward me. "Here, you take old Corpse Finder. Or are you scared, too?" She dangled the turtle over the side boards.

Reaching up as high as I could I took charge of the damn thing.

Brenda shrank back. "It smells awful."

"That thing will find a corpse?" Spoke asked.

"Uh huh."

"Mind telling me how?"

"Snappers eat carrion. It's caviar to them. If there's rotten meat in that pond old Corpse Finder will sniff it out."

Pearl jumped to the turf and with Spoke's assistance lifted the skiff from the pickup and slid it into the water. She tossed the painter to Brenda. "Make sure the boat don't drift away."

Brenda caught the rope, but with a look that implied she wouldn't mind using it to strangle Pearl.

Meanwhile, my arm ached something fierce from holding the snapper.

"Drop that turtle and my Dad will skin you alive."

She hoisted herself onto the pickup, grabbed an oak dowel from a heap of trash, and leapt down beside me. With the dowel she tapped old C.F. on the noggin, none too gently. "To get his attention," she explained. The snapper clamped its jaws onto the wood. "That'll keep him occupied."

Next, she unraveled several feet of cord and threaded the end through a grommet that had been drilled into one of the snapper's serrated plates, just above its tail.

"Fling him into the pond. If there's a cadaver in there Old Corpsey will find it."

Stepping to the water's edge I swung my arm around like a boom and let go of the turtle. When it hit the surface it released the dowel from its jaws and trailing the nylon cord struck out for greater depths.

"What an ugly creature," Brenda whispered. "Its head looks like an uncircumcised penis."

I was rescued from embarrassment by Pearl, who securing the cord's loose end to the skiff's bow said: "I'll need your help."

Spoke approached the skiff.

"Not you," Pearl said. "Him." She pointed to me.

Spoke's Adam's apple bobbed like a cork on a fish line. "I'm in charge of this investigation. Mr. Sullivan is a suspect."

"Him, or go find your own cadaver."

"I should know better than to deal with Starbucks." Throwing his hands up in disgust he stomped back to the cruiser.

I glanced at Brenda—after all, I was getting paid by the hour. For bog work. Not sleuthing.

She tossed the painter into the stern. "Why not?" Even so, she looked none too pleased.

Pearl shoved off. As we drifted lazily from shore she said: "Soon as this cord goes taut you commence to row. I'll tell you which direction."

"How come you wanted me?"

"You're cuter than old Spoke. And bashful. I ain't exactly psychic, but I can tell you're a virgin."

I could feel my face flush crimson, and turned away from her amused expression. Within a few minutes the line tightened.

"Row toward that inlet near them cattails. Quick, before the line fouls on these here stumps."

I dipped the oar blades beneath the surface and like a practiced mariner steered the skiff to where Pearl pointed.

"Better haul in old Corpsey before he chomps off a finger or something." I coiled the slack cord onto the floorboards as she probed the shallows with a gaff.

Glancing over my shoulder, I saw Brenda standing on the dike, next to Spoke, who studied my every move through binoculars. I dragged the snapper to the side of the skiff, where he thrashed about like a bull alligator. "Now what?"

"Let him dangle." Pearl leaned over the bow, the muscles on her slender thighs sculpted like a Remington bronze. When she straightened, a child's sneaker hung from the gaff. She shook the sneaker loose and rammed the gaff into the mud to mark the spot. "Let old Spoke deal with it."

With old C.F. in tow I rowed back to the dike. As we approached within hailing distance Spoke began shouting questions.

"He's there," is all I said.

While the Chief radioed the State Police from his cruiser I helped return the snapper to its crate. As I wiped the slime from my hands Brenda approached. "Chet. Was he…?"

"I didn't get a good look."

"Take the rest of the day off." She touched my hand. "It'll be high tide in an hour or two. What you need is a good swim in clean ocean water. Do you know White Sands?"

I nodded. "It's the beach closest to my room. I can walk there. I don't have a car."

"Hop in. It's too hot to walk."

"Don't wander too far," Spoke shouted, when he saw us climb into the Stealth. "The State Police will have some questions for you."

We were sandwiched between the cruiser and the pickup. As Pearl backed up to give us room, I caught her baleful stare. Was it me, or Brenda, to whom she was giving the Evil Eye?

Brenda dropped me off at Mrs. Kubalski's Guest House. I stood on the curb as she sped off, a black smudge against a blur of cottages and dunes. Across the street the Santos residence—a weathered Cape with dormers, one of them attached to little Bobby's bedroom—stood forlorn. Were the parents at work? Seeking solace from relatives and friends? Actively searching for their son?

I went to my room, showered, donned a swim suit, grabbed a towel and walked down to the beach. In the parking lot splotches of sun glinted off windshields in conspiratorial winks: *We know, even if you don't.*

I swam for awhile, aimlessly, then collapsed onto the towel and fell asleep. I awoke to soft fingers stroking my back.

"Lucky I came along." Brenda continued to rub sun screen onto my shoulders and legs. "You could've got a nasty burn."

Beneath the top of her green two-piece bathing suit the whiteness of her breasts shone like lilies in a field of clover.

"Your turn."

She murmured with contentment as I massaged sun screen onto her thighs. Puffs of cloud momentarily obscured the sun, casting shadows that skimmed along the waves like sharks on the prowl.

"I've got astounding news."

I wiped my hands on the towel and stretched out beside her.

"After I dropped you off I drove back to the bog. I watched as the State Police retrieved the body. Only—" She leaned closer, her nose nearly touching mine—"it wasn't a body."

The sun slid from the clouds; in its rays Brenda's eyes sparkled like many-faceted jewels. "Huh? I saw the body when Pearl Starbuck hooked it with the gaff."

"You saw Bobby Santos's clothes. You didn't see him. Can you believe it? His pants and shirt had been sewn together and stuffed. With dead animals. Road kills, the police say."

I rose on my elbows and stared at her. "Why—?"

She shrugged. "Who can fathom the soul of a psychopath?"

❧∾

In the morning I walked to work as usual, an ocean breeze, like a phantom hand, driving particles of mist across my face. By the time I reached the reservoir the sun's rays had drilled a hole through the fog and I could make out the yellow streamers of crime-scene tape where Corpse Finder had located the smorgasbord of animal cadavers.

On the dike an object loomed like the hull of a wrecked ship: Police Chief Spoke Coffin's blue-and-white. Sans Spoke. Judging by condensation on windows and windshield, the cruiser had sat in the fog several hours.

Had Spoke chosen the spot for a snooze? Wakened in the wee hours to answer a call to nature, lost his way, and foundered in the reservoir?

Dew scintillated on the cranberry vines like precious gems, reminding me of Brenda. And her amethyst eyes, and how we'd kissed and made love in the dying moonlight, on the water-ribbed sand.

The vines too sopping wet to mow, I decided to clean the irrigation ditches instead, a task requiring a potato digger with which to tug weeds from the clogged trenches. I walked along the shore of the bog to the tool shed.

I sensed something wrong when I saw the door to the shed standing ajar. It should have been locked.

When I opened the door the shaft of light exposed Spoke's naked body, smeared in blood, sprawled on the floor. A cowl of congealed gore draped his upper torso. His wrists were cuffed behind his back.

I couldn't see Spoke's head, partly because it was inside the crate, partly because it had been chewed and partially eaten. Old Corpse Finder was inside the crate, too, looking sated and pleased with itself.

Was Spoke dead when introduced to the snapper? Or was old Corpse Finder now Corpse *Maker*?

Staccato bursts of static shattered the rural repose as I figured out how to operate the cruiser's radio. I gave the dispatcher details, then sat on the damp ground and waited.

の

Voluptuous in cotton blouse and shorts, Brenda greeted me with a kiss as I exited the State Police Station in Bourne. "By the way, you're still on the pay roll," she said as she drove me to my room. "It's not your fault bodies keep turning up on Gramps's bog."

We arranged to meet for dinner. In my room, I turned on the A.C. and flopped on the bed and fell immediately asleep, only to be wakened a half hour later by Mrs. Kubalski's stentorian voice hallooing from the first floor. I had a phone call. A young lady.

Expecting Brenda's dulcet tones, I was greeted instead by Pearl Starbuck's nasal twang.

"Chet, don't say nothing."

"What—"

"Shush! The police. They're after me. 'Cause of old Corpse Finder. We gotta talk."

"Wait a sec. I'm in hot water enough as it is."

"Meet me on the dunes back of the old salt works off Braily Road. Make sure nobody follows you." Click.

Damn!

I found Braily Road easily enough, and a ribbon of crumbled asphalt labeled Old Salt Works Road that wended toward the dunes. I followed a footpath into the shifting sands, through mounds of poverty grass shaped like horseshoe crabs, up a steep incline, then down a declivity thick with beach plums and salt spray roses. A sharp dogleg brought me face to face with Pearl Starbuck.

"I knew you'd come." She tore petals from a rose and held them to her cheek. She had on the same cutoffs, this time with a yellow blouse. Her complexion, a pleasing tan, matched the color of the dunes. "We gotta talk fast."

"The police?"

"Uh huh."

"How do you explain what happened?" I asked, the image of Spoke's chewed face fresh in my mind.

"Somebody stole the pickup last night, along with Old Corpsey." The rose petals slipped from her fingers and drifted onto the sand.

I looked into her eyes: brown, flecked with gold. Doe-like. Feral. "Hold on—the police found the pickup parked in your yard."

"The person who stole it brought it back."

"Someone steals a truck, then returns it?"

"It was toward morning. I was awake in bed, listening to the fog horns. I heard an engine, jumped out of bed and peeked out the window. I saw the car when it sped off."

"So tell the police."

"Yeah, sure. They're gonna believe Pearl Starbuck, half-breed."

"This is Massachusetts, not Mississippi."

"Yeah? See if *you* believe me. The car I saw take off: it was that creepy black one of Brenda Rawlings. She must have hidden it nearby when she stole the truck."

The wind coming in off the ocean whipped sand in our faces. I shook my head in disbelief.

"I ain't psychic but I got a sixth sense. She's crazy. She's one of them psychopaths. She has reasons for doing things you or I wouldn't understand."

"Why should I believe you?" Except for a red-tailed hawk circling high overhead we were utterly alone. How easily one of us could murder the other!

She flung her arms around my neck and planted her lips on mine. She smelled of honeysuckle and salt spray roses. "That's why."

I didn't know what to think. Had Brenda indeed stolen the pickup with the snapper and—what? Seduced Spoke? Enticed him into his own handcuffs on the pretext of some sexual game? Then killed him? I couldn't believe that. And yet—I wanted to believe Pearl.

And to complicate matters—I was involved, now, with both women. On top of already being a suspect in the disappearance of little Bobby Santos.

❧

Brenda picked me up at six and drove to a quiet seaside restaurant. On the way I complained of a headache and queasy stomach.

"Overtired, poor dear," she commiserated. "The shock of discovering Chief Coffin's body. And then all those questions from the State Police. Let me take you back to your room."

"Don't fret," Brenda said when she dropped me off. "We'll have lots of other nights together before summer's end."

I pecked her cheek and trudged into the house. A moment later Pearl pulled up in a nondescript Toyota, and I slipped out again, much to the bewilderment of Mrs. Kubalski.

"Where'd you get this heap?" I asked as we screeched from the curb.

"It's my cousin Lenny's. He's in jail, so he lets me use it."

Great. "You expect to keep up with Brenda's Stealth in this?"

"So long as she keeps to back roads, which is what I expect her to do."

We drove to the section of town where the rich folks live and parked across the street and a block down from the Rawlings mansion, an antique Federal that looked more like a museum than a home.

"I'm the crazy one," I muttered.

"I got a hunch she'll venture out again after dark. Hungry? I got ham and cheese, and also tuna."

Night fell. Like a pale tongue licking the earth's fat lip, a sliver of moon shone through thin brush strokes of dark clouds. What kind of sick mind, I wondered, would stuff a missing boy's clothes with dead animals?

I dozed, then awoke with a jolt as the car lurched forward.

"Are you nuts? Switch on the lights!"

"Can't. She might notice and get suspicious. There's enough moon to see by."

And die by, no doubt.

Ahead, red tail lights shone like demon eyes peering through a crack in Hell. We whisked along through swampland and cranberry bogs until a series of twists and turns brought us to an unpaved lane, where the tail lights disappeared around a bend.

"I know where we're at," Pearl said, pulling to a stop. Leaning across my lap she pulled a flashlight from the glove compartment.

We proceeded on foot, fields of cranberry vines surrounding us like an inland sea. A whippoorwill punctured the night with its manic song; before us a shapeless mass gradually assumed the outline of an abandoned building, and next to it, Brenda's Stealth, a perverted Batmobile.

A door next to a loading platform stood ajar. Pearl clicked on the flashlight and we slipped through.

The stench of death smothered the air. Pearl gagged, and I felt the tuna sandwich I'd eaten rise in my gullet.

"No need for Old Corpsey tonight," Pearl whispered.

The beam from the flashlight bobbed through the cobwebs like a gandydancer. The room we found ourselves in was empty, except for the decayed corpse in one corner. Pearl illuminated the face.

"That ain't no twelve-year-old."

Holding my breath I bent over for a closer look. Despite the putrefaction I recognized him. "Hank Rawlings. Brenda's grandfather."

Pearl swept the beam around the empty chamber. "Wonder where she's at."

"I don't know. Let's get out of here."

Pearl seized my arm. "What about the boy. Bobby Santos. He may be alive. We can't leave him here, with *her*."

In a room stacked to the rafters with empty cranberry crates we came upon a flight of steep stairs leading to an attic loft. Rusty scythes and other tools of the cranberry trade lay haphazardly at the foot of the stairs. At the top a shaft of yellow light cut through a crack in the door frame. A soft, eerie crooning issued from behind the door.

"Careful you don't cut yourself," Pearl whispered as she led the way up.

Pearl stood on the landing and tried the knob but found it locked.

"Okay," I said. "Time for some brawn." I heaved my shoulder against the paneled door. On the third try the hinges, with a banshee screech, tore loose and the door flew inward.

Light from a dozen hurricane lamps spilled over us. Blinded, I stood in the threshold and felt Pearl wedge her way in. As my eyes adjusted I saw a cloaked figure hover before me: Brenda. And beyond her a rocking chair, and in it—head lolling like a limp rag—Bobby Santos, all dolled up in a Buster Brown suit.

"Brenda," I shouted.

Costumed like a vampire she looked ludicrous yet beautiful still. As I uttered the last syllable of her name she hurled herself with a shriek against me and clawing at my face knocked me down.

Pearl tore the cloaked figure from me. As I stumbled to my feet I saw them struggle through the ruined doorway onto the landing. As if she was no heavier than a feather pillow Brenda lifted Pearl from the floor and held her above the stairwell. As I lunged forward she tripped on a fold of her cloak and dropping Pearl to one side fell headlong down the steps.

Taking the steps two at a time I rushed to the floor below and found Brenda lying in a heap, a scythe blade through her heart.

I used the cloak as a shroud to cover her body. In the feeble light cast from the room above, her eyes stared wide, unseeing, and I watched the color fade, amethyst to opaque. I knelt by her side and held her hand and felt it grow cold.

After a while Pearl tapped me on the shoulder.

"That little Bobby, he's okay I think. Drugged. She dressed him like a doll and played house with him. I don't see no bite marks. I don't know what kind of vampire she was. Real, or maybe just imagined. I know she was your friend. I'm sorry that she's dead."

I let Brenda's hand fall to the floor. Hugging Pearl, I said, "You're my friend, too." And turning to the stairwell: "Let's hurry that boy home to his folks."

Flume Child

This next one is particularly nasty. Not for the squeamish.

Do you really want to take that nature walk along the dike that bisects

the cranberry bog behind your house? Of course, if your heart is

pure and you say your prayers each night you really

have nothing to fear.

Do you?

SOME FOLKS THINK I'M THE GHOST OF A MURDERED CHILD. Well let me tell you, that's a crock of bull. There ain't no such things as ghosts. I'm flesh and blood same as you. That murdered child they tell about, she was my mom.

My daddy now, he's a no good drifter name of Pete Bartelli. I suppose that makes *me* a Bartelli, despite Pete and mom wasn't married. But believe me, Bartelli's a name I ain't about to take, for reasons I'll explain. Pete Bartelli may be my daddy but that don't mean I got to call myself after him.

If I had to choose a name for myself I guess it would be Flume Child. That's what most folks hereabouts call me. Flume Child. It's as good a name as any, even though the people who call me it think I'm a spirit from the dead.

Pete Bartelli was only seventeen years of age when he fathered me. But that ain't no excuse for what he done. Last winter he turned thirty. I know enough about figuring to know that makes me thirteen years old. Thirteen is still a child, even though I don't feel still a child. Sometimes I feel like I'm a hundred years old, same as these here cranberry bogs. And sometimes I feel like the bogs...like *they* are my real parents.

But what I feel don't matter much, I guess.

Even so, I'm glad my daddy come back to these parts. Some folks— if they knew the facts—might call it fate that me and him should meet for the first time on the anniversary of my mom's death. Well, I can tell you it wasn't no fate. I planned it that way. There ain't much that goes on here that I don't know about. Just because I never been to school don't mean I'm ignorant. I know the exact day and year my mom was murdered. And when Pete Bartelli drifted back into town I heard about that, too.

I keep in touch. The bogs ain't so deep in the woods that I can't sneak into town every so often. Sometimes I'll sneak into town three or four nights in a row, especially if it's real stormy. When the wind comes howling through the trees and the rain slats hard against the window panes people stay put—a good time for me to come out, when nobody can't see me.

The flumes is where I live. In case you don't know a flume, it's a shaft made from concrete and oak planks built into a dike to let water flow from one section of cranberry bog to another. It's real comfortable in the flumes. Every day I pick a different flume to sleep in. I curl up in the mud at the bottom of the shaft. It's cool down there. Damp. I like the damp. And the quiet. What I especially like is the dark.

The dark is my friend.

When it's real dark I crawl out, and that's how come they know to call me Flume Child. A couple of times I been spotted climbing in or out. It was bog workers who seen me. They got nosy and tried to poke around. Well let me tell you, I fixed them. I fixed them good. Nobody ain't ever come back for a second look.

The place in town I like best to visit is where my mom used to live. It's a little white house with a white picket fence stuck all by itself at the end of a winding road. I been inside that house lots of times—late at night when the lady who lives there was fast asleep. That lady, Mrs. Sullivan, is my mom's mom. That makes me Mrs. Sullivan's granddaughter, I guess, though she ain't never seen me and don't know I exist. If she ever seen me she'd be scared, I guess.

Mr. Sullivan now, he's dead. They say he died from grief when his only child was murdered. Her name by the way was Cathy.

Sometimes I call myself Cathy Flume Child, after my mom.

Like I said, I never been to school. Even so, I got ways of learning. I listen outside people's windows. Folks say all sorts of things when they think no one else can't hear. And I learn from TV when nobody is home. There ain't many houses in this town I ain't been inside of one time or another.

There ain't many secrets I don't know.

That's how I figured out who killed my mom. And that's how I found out when my daddy was back in town. I overheard Bert Howland tell his wife, "That no good Pete Bartelli is back. Shacked up with Sally Morrell." In case you don't know, Sally is the local whore. She lives in a dilapidated shanty on Maple Street across from the lumber yard.

And sure enough, that's where I found my daddy, in bed with Sally. It was late and they was both asleep.

Now, I should tell you that when they found my mom's body it was at the bottom of a flume. That's where Pete Bartelli flung her, after he raped her and choked her to death. She wasn't but seven years old when he killed her. She lay in the mud many long months before the bog workers come upon her.

You might be asking yourself, how can a seven-year-old child—a *dead* seven-year-old child—be somebody's mom? Well let me tell you, it's a fact. Pete Bartelli, he raped her, and maybe it was some chemical in the bog water what done it, but whatever it was it caused her to give birth even though she was dead, and what she gave birth to was me. I know that to be a fact, because I ain't no ghost. There ain't no such thing as a ghost. I'm flesh and blood, same as you.

Even though I'm flesh and blood I never but once showed myself on purpose to anybody. That one time was last night, the anniversary of my mom's death.

It was after midnight, bitter cold, the wind howling through the trees, the moon bright as a jacko'lantern in the sky. But that didn't bother me none. I crept around to the back of Sally's shack—her yard is messy, she don't never mow the grass and nobody could see me amongst the weeds— and tapped at the bedroom window to wake my daddy up.

It was Sally who rolled herself out of bed and staggered over to the window. She didn't have no clothes on. She fumbled with the pane until finally she got it open.

"Whaddya want? I got someone here with me." Her eyes were red, kind of unfocused.

Then I guess she saw me. She started to scream.

My daddy, he kicked the covers aside and sprung out of bed. He didn't have no clothes on neither.

I took hold of the sill and hoisted myself in.

Sally, she turned whiter than a sheet and shrunk back into a corner, biting on the knuckles of her hand until the skin broke and blood began to flow, all the time screaming.

My daddy, he just stood there, naked, in the middle of the room sort of swaying like. I could smell he had been drinking but I guess the sight of me sobered him some.

"Christ!"

"Daddy."

It was like one of them scenes on TV when father and daughter meet for the first time.

"Daddy."

He didn't budge, so I took the first step. I flung my arms around him and planted a kiss square on his lips.

He went crazy. There ain't no other way to describe what he done. He started to beat on me with his fists.

"Daddy."

He tried to push me off but I clung to him. He started in to punching me again. Then when I wouldn't let go he grabbed hold of my throat and begun to squeeze, hard.

I guess I sort of went crazy, too. After all I am only flesh and blood and what he done to me hurt. I bit into his lips and tore them off with my teeth. Then I reached up and scratched out his eyes.

He started to scream along with Sally, only his screams was bubbly with blood.

I could of stopped there but I didn't. I reached down and fixed him so he won't rape nobody, never again.

Maybe you think I oughtn't to have done that. Because he is my daddy.

Well, he deserved it. For what he done to my mom.

For what he done to me.

Mock Turtle Soup

There are those who, upon reading this story, will ask: but where is the ghost? Others having read the story will only nod their head and say to themselves: ah, then it is true! Hauntings can take many shapes, many forms.

One thing is certain: the author's fascination with snapping turtles remains unabated.

"He beat her so badly she lost the sight of one eye." Laura held up the photograph and angled it so that Frank could examine it while continuing to drive.

The dirt track snaked like an old Indian trail (which in all probability it had been at one time) through terrain that was half forest, half swampland. As the car lurched along Frank allowed his gaze to shift for a moment to the black and white glossy. The face attached to the unconscious form sprawled on the emergency-room gurney seemed scarcely human.

"I'm surprised she lived."

"She nearly didn't. He cracked four of her ribs and fractured her skull."

He nodded toward the photo. "How'd you get hold of that?"

"It was presented as evidence at the trial. The prosecutor gave Kate a copy. Don't ask me why." Laura braced herself against the dashboard as the car jounced over a deep rut. "Later, when I took a psych course in college I wrote a paper on battered women. Kate let me interview her. With hindsight, I now realize how painful it must have been for her to talk about it. Cousin Kate's a very private person."

"She won't have any problems maintaining her privacy if she doesn't do something about this road. We should have rented a Jeep."

"It isn't much farther. Anyhow, that's how I got the photo. If she suspects I've shown it to you she'll have a fit."

Frank glanced at the stark image. "It isn't very flattering. What'd he use—a baseball bat?"

"His fists."

"And now he's been released from prison?"

"Uh huh."

"And the purpose of our visit is to persuade your cousin Kate to move in with you?"

"For a while at least. To get her out of harm's way. In case he comes looking for her."

"Suppose he tracks her down, to your apartment? You'd both be in danger."

Laura shrugged. "I'll take that risk. Kate will be a lot safer in the city than she would be, all alone, out here. That is, *if* she consents to make the move."

She fell silent. Moments later the road debouched into a clearing, beyond which lay acres of cranberry bog—low sunken fields of burgundy-colored vines draped over the earth like plush carpeting. In the distance, at the edge of a swamp, a clapboard house in antique yellow with a steeply pitched gambrel roof stood high on a knoll overlooking the bog. Wisps of smoke curled from the chimney, gray smears against the bright October sky.

"Stop the car," Laura said. "I want to enjoy the view. It's been a long time since I last saw the bogs. When I was little my grandparents lived here, along with Kate and my aunt and uncle. They're all dead now. All except for Kate."

From the shallows of the man-made reservoir that supplied the cranberry bog with water for irrigation a blue heron lifted into the air, dragging its long legs skyward. Lean and lanky, it flapped its massive wings with an easy grace, then drifted out of sight behind a clump of cattails.

"It's so peaceful," Laura said.

"Yeah. And isolated."

Frank started the engine and they continued along the dirt track, which skirted the bog as it curved upward toward the house. A chunk of the knoll, eaten away by years of excavation, showed signs of recent digging.

"What's been going on over there?" Frank pointed to several acres of scarred land where the ground had been gouged by heavy equipment.

"That's the sand pit. Cranberry vines have to be coated with a layer of sand every so often. Kate has two men working full time. Each fall they spend a few weeks spreading sand over sections of bog that need it."

"So she's not entirely alone out here."

"She is at night. And most weekends."

The road twisted to an abrupt halt on a gravel apron that was bordered by lawn. A walkway paved with crushed sea shells—which crunched under their shoes like brittle bones—led to the house. Huge, ancient rhododendrons stood guard at each side of the front door.

As they walked up to the steps Laura suddenly gripped Frank's arm. Wordlessly, she stooped and retrieved an object from the grass.

"What is it?"

She showed him an empty nip bottle, then slipped it into her coat pocket.

"Is your cousin Kate a boozer?"

"Don't be a jerk, Frank."

"Hey, I only asked. Given her history of abuse…"

"It's Jim Beam. *He* drinks Jim Beam." She gripped the metal knocker and gave a couple of brisk raps.

Almost immediately Kate opened the door. She greeted them with a smile. "Come and sit in the living room. I've got a nice fire going."

She hugged Laura and gave Frank a warm handshake and ushered them into a spacious room where, in a tiled corner, a Franklin stove stood with open hearth. A calico cat, stretched full length on a scatter rug before the stove, was taking advantage of the heat. Half a dozen hooked or braided rugs gave the room the comfortable, homey feeling of old New England. The delicious odor of something cooking permeated the air.

Kate took their coats and disappeared into another part of the house.

"Millions of people—both guys *and* gals—drink Jim Beam," Frank said with lowered voice.

"Out here?" Laura shook her head decisively. "I distinctly remember Kate telling me how she used to give him Jim Beam collector bottles on his birthdays and Christmas. And how he smashed them all in a drunken rage the day he beat her and almost killed her. He's been here. I'm convinced of it."

Kate returned moments later with a tray laden with a decanter and wine glasses. As the three of them sat sipping chilled Chablis and chatting about the weather, Frank studied his hostess. He could see little family resemblance between Laura and her cousin.

Kate was shorter, five feet two to Laura's five five. And darker. Laura had soft brown hair and green eyes—not unusual for Portuguese stemming from the Azores—whereas Kate was favored with the classic olive complexion of the mainland Portuguese, and black, thick hair and sloe eyes. One of those eyes was disfigured with a permanent cast, compliments of her ex-husband. She appeared to be somewhere in her late thirties, ten or twelve years older than Laura.

As if aware of his scrutiny Kate turned to Frank and said: "Laura tells me you're a detective."

"That's right. More precisely a fraud investigator. For the Department of Public Welfare."

"Sounds like fascinating work. You must meet all kinds."

"That I do."

"He met *me*." Laura reached over and patted his knee.

"I met Laura while investigating a case of fraud at the nursing home where she works," Frank explained.

"Well, I think it's sweet of Laura to want you to meet *me*."

"It's not the only reason why we're here," Laura confessed.

"No?" Kate lifted the decanter and carefully poured herself another glass of wine.

Laura toyed with her own half-filled glass. "Kate, I'm worried. About you. Living out here, alone, in the middle of nowhere."

"Now that he's been released you mean."

"Yes."

Kate tossed back her head and gave a loud laugh.

The action, so unexpected, startled Frank.

"I'm not a woman to beat on twice."

"I know. It's just that—"

"I feel perfectly safe," her cousin interjected. "And I'll show you why." She got up from her chair and left the room.

Laura shot Frank an anguished look. "Damn! I'm not handling this well."

"If you two were to live together you'd be at each other's throat." He quaffed what was left of his Chablis.

"That's not true. Right now Kate's under a great deal of stress."

"Which, if she moved into your apartment, you'd be sharing."

Kate cut short their argument by reappearing in the room. "This is my protection," she declared, brandishing a revolver.

Though careful to keep the barrel pointed away from her guests she was obviously nervous, on edge.

Frank gave Laura a reassuring pat. To Kate: "A .38 Special. An old stand-by. May I see it?" He rose from his seat and strolled over to where she was standing.

He held out his hand.

She hesitated, as if reluctant to relinquish a cherished memento. Then gave it to him.

"Careful. It's loaded."

"So I see."

He examined the weapon, saw that it had been recently cleaned.

"It's well cared for." He handed it back. "You obviously know something about firearms."

"Shouldn't everyone these days? Certainly a woman who lives alone."

She laid the revolver on the top shelf of a mahogany bookcase. She allowed her hand to linger above the weapon for a moment or two then abruptly crossed over to the stove, selected a chunk of split maple from the wood box, and shoved it into the fire.

Switching her tail, the calico glared up from the rug and gave a plaintive meow.

"Poor Buttons. She dislikes guns." She stooped and stroked the cat's smooth fur, and added wood to the fire.

"Guns make me nervous, too," Laura said.

"Then we won't talk about them." Kate returned to her chair. "Let's finish our wine, then have lunch. I've cooked something very special for you two."

"Sure smells delicious," Frank said. "Can Laura and I help?"

"With what? Lunch? Or my general well-being?"

"Lunch," Laura declared. She drained the remaining drops form her glass and sat silent for a moment. As if to ward off a chill she went over to the stove, stood before the open flame, and rubbed her hands together.

Kate gathered up the empty glasses and carried them into the kitchen.

"And I haven't even asked her to move in yet," Laura said, more to herself than to Frank.

"Just make sure she's not pointing the gun at you when you do."

"Frank! You can be so crude!"

He crossed the room and stood by her side. He ruffled her hair and gently kissed her cheek. "Let's go see what's cooking. I'm starved."

They found Kate standing in the kitchen before a gas range. She was stirring, with a wooden spoon, the contents of a huge cauldron from which fragrant steam billowed in roiling clouds.

"Mmm," Frank said. "Doesn't look like laundry. Must be lunch."

"And it's just about ready." Kate removed the spoon from the scalding liquid and pointed with it over her shoulder. "The table's all set. Sit down and be comfortable. I'll join you in a minute."

She dipped the spoon into the pot, withdrew it brimming, and held it to her lips. Blowing on the hot broth before tasting it she said: "I hope you don't mind the informality. It's cozier in here than in the dining room. And the view is nicer. I've seated you both so that you can look out over the bog."

"There must be something I can help with," Laura said.

"I've got Portuguese rolls warming in the oven, which you can take out and cover in a basket. But that's about it. Everything else is under control." She shut off the burner and placed a heavy lid on the pot. "There's one more thing I want to attend to. I'll be right back."

She disappeared into the living room. Frank plunked himself at the table while Laura slid into a pair of hand-woven oven mitts and saw to the Portuguese rolls.

When Kate returned from the living room she was holding the revolver.

"I believe it was Chekov who said that if you show a gun in Act One it had damn well better go off in Act Three. Or something to that effect."

She twisted the revolver in her hand, all the while staring at it in the manner of Lady Macbeth, as if imagining powder burns on her hands in place of blood.

"Oh, I'm not going to shoot myself if that's what you're thinking. I'm merely putting it away—so that it *doesn't* go off."

She left the room again. This time they heard a drawer open and close.

When Kate returned she said: "There. That's done. Now for lunch."

She removed the lid from the pot and began to ladle the contents into a large tureen. "Help yourselves to wine from the decanter. And pour me a glass." She carried the tureen to the table and from it filled their plates.

"You're right about the view," Frank said. "Look! There goes a hawk."

"A pair of them hangs out in that stand of pines behind the sand pit." She seated herself, plucked a roll from the basket, and without further ceremony began to eat.

"Kate, I have to say, this soup is delicious!" Laura exclaimed.

"I hope you don't mind. Nothing fancy. Just soup and bread."

"Mind?" Frank said. "This soup is more like a stew. Chock full of all the tasty goodies *I* need."

"For dessert we'll have slices of melon with cheese," Kate said.

They enjoyed their food in silence for a while.

"Kate," Laura finally asked, "What kind of meat is this? It doesn't taste like chicken, and it's certainly not ham or beef. So tender. I just can't seem to identify it."

Her cousin chuckled. "See if you can guess. I'll give you a clue. I got the recipe from an old Fannie Farmer Cook Book I picked up at a yard sale last summer. It's called Mock Turtle Soup. I did cheat a little, though. I didn't follow the recipe *exactly*.

"Whatever you did I wouldn't mind having seconds," Frank said. "Okay if I help myself?"

Without waiting for permission he reached over to the tureen and filled his plate.

Kate smiled. "I like to see a man eat."

"I'm the same way," Laura said. "It comes from being Portuguese."

"*He* didn't care much for food. He'd rather drink."

"Jim Beam, wasn't it?"

"For starters. Once he got going anything would do. Cheap whiskey. Cheap wine. Anything."

"Kate." Laura reached over and took her cousin's hand. "I don't want to frighten you. But you ought to know. I found a Jim Beam bottle near the walkway."

"Why should that frighten me?"

"Don't you see? It means he's been here. He might come back. He—"

"Might hurt me? No." Kate shook her head. "Oh no. I swore he'd *never* lay a hand on me again and I meant it. This—" she pointed to her blind eye—"is a daily reminder. I don't need any Jim Beam bottle."

"But…you live here all alone."

"That's not true. I've got Buttons."

"A cat!"

"And," Kate cocked her head in the direction of the door through which she'd exited earlier, "I've got my .38 Special."

"Kate, Laura would like you to move in with her for a while."

She turned a livid face to him. "What? Leave my house? And my livelihood? Don't be silly. Those two morons who work for me know less about cranberries than Buttons does. They'd have me bankrupt in a week if I didn't keep an eye on them." She raised her hand to her blind eye. "No pun intended."

"At least think about it," Laura said.

"You're worrying about me for nothing. Not that I don't appreciate your concern." Kate went around to the younger woman and gave her a hug. "Look. Through this window. A panoramic view of the cranberry bog and the only road that leads to it. I spotted your car long before you reached the house."

"But you were expecting us. And you can't sit here and look out the window twenty-four hours a day. At night it's pitch black out there. I know. All those times I slept over as a child. Remember?"

"Yes, I remember. I was like a big sister to you, wasn't I? More than just a cousin."

"More than just my *favorite* cousin. That's why I wish you'd—"

"But Laura, you haven't been listening! Look, here's the scenario. Picture this happening, will you? I'm sitting here in the kitchen at this very table. It's just before dark—but I haven't turned the lights on yet. It's so quiet and peaceful as the day fades! I've had my supper, washed and dried the dishes and put them away. Though I have a book before me I'm not really reading. I'm day dreaming, gazing out over the bog watching the shadows creep in from the swamp. Can you picture all this? Buttons curled in the corner by her dish, too lazy to seek out a warmer spot by the wood stove."

"Sounds idyllic," Frank admitted. "Meanwhile your soup is growing cold."

"But I told you, I've already had my supper!"

"He means the soup in front of you now," Laura said.

"Forget that. I can warm it up later. Right now I want you to understand why I'm perfectly safe. Here. In my own house. Now listen!

"It's twilight, remember. I must have dozed off, for suddenly I hear the crunch of footsteps on the walkway. Those oyster shells—they're my early warning system. I wake with a start, peer through the pane, see that it's *him*.

"What do I do? Panic? Go hide in my closet? Of course not. This is *my* house. *My* domain. Calmly, I fetch my revolver from the drawer, check to see that it's loaded, and wait for his knock. When I hear it I go to the door.

"'Yes?'

"'Kate, it's me.'

"'What do you want?'

"'Kate. I want to talk to you.'"

She paused. "Well, the conversation goes something like that. I say, 'Go away. You're not wanted here.'

"But he won't go away. He becomes angry, pounds on the door, kicks it, tries to break it down. I say, 'Okay. Okay. I'll let you in,' and I open the door. And shoot him. Twice. In the chest. He falls bleeding over the threshold. I stand holding the door open, and watch him slowly die."

"Oh Kate, how horrible!"

"Do you see how simple it is? I tell you, I'm perfectly safe here."

Frank stared at her. Then said: "But now you have a body to dispose of."

"There are hundreds of ways to dispose of a body."

"Frank! Kate isn't really going to shoot anyone, no matter how much they may deserve it." Laura's eyes flashed with annoyance—followed by a flicker of doubt. "But if she ever did shoot someone, it would be in self-defense."

"They might not believe me," Kate said. "A jury, I mean. They might say I could have somehow avoided killing him. They might say I didn't try hard enough to run away. And then they'd try to convict me of manslaughter. Why should I go to jail because of *him*? Why should I even have to stand trial?"

"Oh Kate!" Laura rose from the table and flung her arms around her cousin. "Don't torture yourself with such thoughts. Come stay with me. For a few weeks at least. I can take time off from work. We'll go shopping, talk about old times—and you can cook once in a while. I love your cooking, Kate."

During this display of emotion Frank sat leaning on his elbows gazing out the window.

"Plenty of places to hide a body, that's for sure. The sand pit, for instance. Easy digging. And whose suspicions would be aroused by recently disturbed earth? Nobody's. It would be like Poe's 'Purloined Letter.' A spot so obvious no one would think to look there."

"Stop acting like a detective," Laura said. To Kate: "Will you show me that recipe for Mock Turtle Soup? I still haven't figured out what kind of meat you used. Not pork. Veal maybe?"

"Now who's being a detective?" Frank quipped. "The case of the mysterious meat."

"Maybe not so mysterious after all," Kate said, an enigmatic smile curling her lips. Leaving the table she slid a well-worn volume from a shelf and handed it to Laura. "Page one hundred and twenty-seven."

Laura cradled the book in her hands and admired it. "*The Boston Cooking-School Cook Book* by Fannie Merritt Farmer. Printed in 1912." She flipped though the pages. "Here it is. Mock Turtle Soup. Oh, it calls for Madeira wine."

"Ah," Frank said. "Madeira. That accounts for the rich flavor."

"And all sorts of spices. Cloves, peppercorns, thyme. Lemon juice. Frank, you'll never guess what the meat is!" Before he could reply she blurted out: "Calf's head. Can you imagine that? Kate, where in the world did you find a calf's head?"

Laying the book face-down on the table she hurried over to the pot and reached for the lid. "Is it still in there? Whatever does it look like?"

"No!" Kate cried out. "Don't peek!" She lunged from the table and seized Laura's hand. "Don't peek," she repeated, as she pulled Laura away from the stove.

Stunned, Laura slowly disengaged from her cousin's grip. She cast a distressed glance toward Frank, who stood by the window with the detached air of someone who has just moments ago witnessed a serious accident.

Kate sank into the nearest chair. "I'm sorry." She brushed her hand over her eyes in a gesture of utter weariness. "I didn't mean to over-react. I've been under so much strain. And you still haven't guessed correctly." Attempting a smile she explained: "It isn't a calf's head. I told you I hadn't followed the recipe exactly. I substituted something for the calf's head. Something very special."

Frank cleared his throat. "What did you substitute?"

"I—" She hesitated. "I guess it really doesn't matter, does it? This elaborate charade. Mock Turtle Soup. What a joke!" She fell silent, folded her hands on her lap, and gazed out the window.

Frank walked over to the still steaming pot and lifted the lid. With the wooden spoon he stirred the contents and probed around inside.

Laura watched, until she could no longer contain herself.

"For God's sake, what is it?"

Frank shrugged. "Can't tell."

Kate let out a high-pitched laugh, a near cackle. "That's right, how could you?" She got up from her chair and began to pace.

Turning to Frank, she said: "You thought it was him, didn't you? That you'd find *his* head in there." She lifted the cook book off the table and waved it above her head. "It's true that I'm stressed out. But I'm not crazy."

Hesitant, Laura approached her, then threw her arms around her. "Don't talk nonsense. We don't think you're crazy."

"I used *a real turtle*," Kate explained. "That was the joke. A *real* turtle for *Mock* Turtle Soup."

With the tips of her fingernails she tapped the book's cover. "The instructions for cooking terrapin are in here." She leafed through the pages until she came upon the section she sought. "'Plunge into boiling water and boil five minutes.' They mean a live terrapin, of course. But I was merciful. I first cut off the head. With an ax.

"'Remove skin from feet and tail by rubbing with a towel.' My turtle was too tough for that. An old snapper. I had to use pliers to pull off the skin. 'Put in a kettle, cook until meat is tender.' After you cook it you 'cut nails from feet' and remove the shell. I think I'll use the shell as a doorstop. After it's had a chance to dry and the smell has gone. Maybe I'll even paint a design on it. Something floral. An interesting conversation piece, don't you think?"

Frank quietly returned to his seat near the window. "Did you catch the turtle yourself?"

"Of course. The swamp is full of snappers. They're forever crawling along the dikes. Sometimes you have to stop your car to avoid running over them."

"I remember, now," Laura said. "Grandfather used to eat snapping turtles. He'd catch them and kill them, just like you said. By cutting off their head with an ax. How Grandmother hated to cook them!"

"She hated to cook eels, too," Kate said. "Grandmother was squeamish. She didn't like the way the eels seemed to squirm in the frying pan, even though they had been skinned, and were obviously dead."

"I'm amazed at how sweet the turtle meat tastes," Frank said. "I would expect a creature that spends its life in the swamp to have a gamey taste."

"Ah, there's a secret to that. You keep the turtle in a barrel for two or three months and feed it on table scraps."

"That sounds cruel," Laura said.

"Cruel? There's nothing cruel about it. Where do snapping turtles spend most of their time? Why, buried in the mud, at the bottom of some pond or ditch. That is, when they're not busy killing ducks or baby geese. Plunk them under a heap of garbage and they're happy as pigs in shit. The garbage fattens them up, and gets rid of the wild taste, all at the same time. If only life for the rest of us were that easy! Eat garbage, and purge yourself of all the bitterness."

"Don't you think you need a change from all of this?" Laura asked. "I know you don't mind living alone. But sometimes it helps to be around people now and then, if only for a week or two."

Kate glanced at Frank. "She doesn't understand, does she?"

"Understand what? What are you taking about? Frank, what is she talking about?"

"In the end," Kate said sadly, "Chekov is right. At some point the gun has to go off. But sometimes it doesn't happen during the play. Sometimes the gun has already been fired. Long before the play begins."

"Where is he?" Frank asked.

"In the sand pit. Where else? You were right. Who would give a second thought to freshly dug ground in a sand pit?"

"Then what you described was real?" Laura said. "He came to the door and tried to break in and you shot him?"

"Yes."

"And afterwards you buried him in the sand pit?" Laura seized her cousin's hands. "No one has to know. We won't tell, will we, Frank? It'll be our little secret. We'll pretend you never told us."

Kate shook her head. "I've tried. It's not working. I can't live with a skeleton. Pretty soon I'd be imagining things. I'd be hearing his steps, at night, on the walkway. I'd be glancing out the window expecting his ghost to appear. I'd be seeing him—with my blind eye."

"It was self-defense. You acted in self-defense. He deserved to die."

"Yes. He deserved to die. Maybe I can convince a jury of that. Maybe they'll be lenient with me." She rose from her seat. "I'll phone the police. Then we'll clear the table. How's that sound?"

The Haunted Screenhouse

The silence of the house began to impress him

disagreeably. He looked behind him and about him,

hoping, and yet fearing, that something

would break the stillness.

—Algernon Blackwood,

"A CASE OF EAVESDROPPING"

THE FIRST THING THE BOYS CAME UPON when they emerged from the swamp was a derelict hand pump. Although they were thirsty from having tramped through the woods all afternoon, the pump promised no relief. Its cast iron spout and handle were sadly rusted, its leathers cracked and flaked to nothingness. Shards of glass lying half buried in the soil at the base of the pipe to which the pump was attached seemed to mock their predicament; the shards were all that remained of the jar that, decades ago, would have held water for priming.

Beyond the pump loomed the hulk of a deserted screenhouse.

It was the isolation—the building's location, rather than any architectural feature or disfigurement brought on by age, weather, or neglect—that made it appear so sinister. The clearing at the edge of the swamp upon which the screenhouse stood was miles from any habitation. The rutted dirt track leading up to it was overgrown with weeds and red cedar saplings, sure sign of abandonment. Even so, the screenhouse, which had withstood more than a century's worth of the worst that New England could hurl at it by way of nor'easter or hurricane, looked to be in remarkably good condition. The roof sagged no more than was to be expected for a building which was at least a hundred years old but had been kept in good repair for the first two-thirds of its existence; most of its roof shingles were intact, as were all of its windows. No clapboards hung loose; no rampant vines with invasive tendrils clung to its walls.

The boys walked around the building twice. They tried the doors but found them locked. They peered in through windows streaked with grime and saw stacks of wooden bushel boxes which in the old days had been used for harvesting cranberries, old tools, and antiquated equipment whose purpose was a mystery to them.

"It'd be neat to poke around inside," Christopher said. Like his companion he was twelve. He had never properly explored an abandoned building, let alone a screenhouse.

"It's haunted," Raymond said.

"Sure looks it."

"No, really. This is the Thompson bog. Everyone knows their screenhouse is haunted."

"You been here before?"

Raymond shook his head. "I never been this far through the swamp. I've rid my bike on the tar road, though." He nodded east, across the vast acreage of cranberry vines. No paved road was visible but Christopher took his friend's word that one was there. "Joey Ramos told me about the ghost. And Kevin Murdock, too. Everybody knows about this place."

"What kind of ghost?" Christopher demanded.

Raymond shrugged. "A ghost. That's all I know."

"Aw, it's just a story."

Raymond kicked idly at a stone but remained silent.

The two boys lingered, each reluctant to suggest leaving and thereby give the impression of being scared. Both were secretly glad that the locked doors provided a plausible excuse not to venture inside.

"We better head home," Christopher said, finally, after they had loitered a decent interval. "I promised my mom I wouldn't be late."

"We can go by the road," Raymond said. "It's shorter. We gotta hurry, though."

⤟⤞

Christopher made it home just in time for supper. When asked about his day, he told of the trek through the swamp but omitted any mention of the screenhouse. After supper he helped with the dishes then went to up to his room, where he read for a while before turning off the light. Tuckered out from having walked so many miles, he closed his eyes and immediately fell asleep. He dreamt of the screenhouse. In the dream he was by himself; it was broad daylight and he stood on his tiptoes peering in through one of the windows. At first all he saw were cobwebs and shadows and dust motes. But as he strained his eyes to see better, one of the shadows moved. It wasn't really a shadow, he realized, but instead a mass of filth-encrusted cobwebs—draped over an invisible form, like a shroud.

The shroud or the thing beneath the shroud detached itself from the other shadows and hovered for a while like a giant moth before drifting—floating—through the cluttered interior of the screenhouse toward the window at which he was peering in. It moved slowly, though with apparent purpose; Christopher felt himself the manifest object of its intent. Panic seized him. He attempted to tear himself away from the window but was unable to; his hands refused to loosen their grip on the sill, as if his fingers were glued to it. In his frenzy to break free he arched his head backwards, like a devotee offering his own throat for sacrifice. The floating shroud edged closer, all the way up to his face, until nothing more than a fragile pane of glass prevented it from touching him.

The shroud, he saw, had a mask, or face, of its own.

Christopher woke up screaming.

๛

Two nights later he had a similar dream. In this version, however, he found himself inside the screenhouse, in the pitch black of night, groping blindly among the shadows. He could sense a presence inside the room other than his own. As he lurched around among the stored objects frantically seeking a way out, soft, unidentifiable things—strips of foul-smelling cloth, like cerements torn from a corpse; or the tips of bat wings; or puffs of putrid air—brushed against his naked face and outstretched hands. Mercifully, he willed himself to waken before the ghost or whatever it was discovered his whereabouts and seized hold of him.

The nightmares continued, intermittently, throughout the rest of the summer. Though they did not occur nightly, or even weekly, when they did occur they were shockingly vivid, the more terrifying in that they seldom followed the same script. Sometimes Christopher found himself inside the screenhouse, sometimes without. Sometimes the haunting presence was seen, at other times only felt. Always, though, he was alone, helpless, overwhelmed by dread.

He confided in no one. It was an overactive imagination, he supposed, that caused the nightmares. He had listened to ghost stories before, of course, dozens of times, around camp fires in the summer, at Halloween parties, or even on Christmas Eve at his grandparents'. He had seen countless horror movies, at the cinema and on television, classics like *Frankenstein* and *Dracula*, as well as the more modern, more graphic flics. None of these had ever given him nightmares. No monster born of fable or film had ever kept him awake at night or haunted his dreams. Why, then, should the ghost in the Thompson screenhouse so disturb his sleep?

Was it because this ghost might be real and not, like the others, fiction or make-believe?

If he could somehow learn the full story behind the ghost—if he could even just know for a fact that the ghost was real and not merely a figment—he could lay it to rest, easily; of that he felt confident.

෴

He saw Raymond only occasionally. The boys, though friends, and happy to spend a few hours together now and then, were by no means best buddies. Raymond liked sports: baseball, basketball, even football. Christopher preferred to go out into the countryside exploring, to hunt for arrowheads or look for frogs and turtles. Or he was content to spend long hours at home reading. On those few occasions that summer when he spent time with Raymond, he did not refer to the screenhouse or the ghost. He hoped that his friend, without prompting, would bring up the subject on his own. But Raymond, too, was reticent. It could be that, like Christopher, he was having nightmares, and for fear of sounding like a wimp didn't want to talk about them. More likely, though, he had forgotten all about the ghost.

Christopher thought that if he returned to the screenhouse by himself and spent an hour or two exploring the building the nightmares might cease. In late August, a few days before school started up again, he rode his bicycle along the winding back roads that led to the Thompson bog. It was the middle of the week; when he got to the dirt road that led up to the screenhouse he discovered a crew of men working there. From a distance he could see a tractor crawling along a dike, mowing the tall grass and weeds, and two or three workers treading over the vines doing something with the irrigation system. They were obviously getting ready for the fall harvest. Half disappointed, half relieved, he turned around and pedaled home.

The nightmares stopped after awhile, only to resume, sporadically, the following summer. It was as though his subconscious (he knew about such things from reading books and watching television) was telling him, *it may have been inconvenient to flout the ghost during the winter, but now it's summertime once more; go back and give it another try.* But after his experience of the previous year—when he had to turn back because of the workers but was glad for it—he was reluctant to return to the screenhouse alone.

Enough time had elapsed, he thought, for him to safely bring up the subject of the ghost again with Raymond. On a damp, overcast day in late June he sought his friend out and suggested, offhandedly, that since the weather wasn't much good for anything else, why not explore the old Thompson screenhouse?

"It'll be a fun thing to do. Maybe we'll get to see that ghost you were telling me about," he said casually.

"It's private property," Raymond objected. "It's posted with 'no trespassing' signs. We could get into trouble."

"We won't touch anything. Just poke around."

"The doors are kept locked. We'd have to break in somehow," Raymond said. "That's illegal."

Though Christopher knew better than to openly taunt his friend with the accusation that he might be afraid of the ghost, he hinted as much. Raymond grew sullen and suggested that he had better things to do than ride his bike halfway across town just to breathe in the dust of a dirty old screenhouse. It wasn't raining yet; if Christopher wanted to join him in shooting a few baskets, fine. Otherwise he could just watch, or do as he liked.

❧

Having failed to enlist the aid of his friend, Christopher tried a different tack. He sought out Joey Ramos and Kevin Murdock, the guys who, Raymond said, had told him about the alleged ghost in the first place.

With each boy in turn Christopher brought up the subject of the haunted screenhouse as if it had been a recent discovery of his. Could there really be a ghost? If so, what kind of ghost? Wouldn't it be neat to sneak inside and see for themselves!

Joey, who at fifteen was two years older than Christopher, scoffed at the notion of what he called "spooks." Fortunately there were no other kids around to serve as audience, else he might have given Christopher a hard time. "That's just something the older guys made up to scare little kids at Halloween." He looked at Christopher scornfully. "You actually believe in that stuff?"

Kevin, who was a year younger than Christopher, balked at the idea of a ghost-hunting expedition. His reason? He wasn't interested, that was all. Though obviously ashamed to admit it, the idea seemed to make him nervous. When pressed for details regarding the nature of the haunting, he could only shrug his shoulders and say that everyone knew the screenhouse was haunted.

If he were to persist in pestering his friends about the ghost, Christopher knew, word would soon get around and he would become the butt of jokes. His best hope now for learning more was to bide his time until Halloween; no one could fault him for bringing up the topic during that ghoulish holiday. In the meantime he would try to wean his mind from things macabre by pursuing other interests, such as a recently discovered pastime, bottle picking. In his cross-country ramblings he had come across two or three old cellar holes deep in the woods whose dump sites promised to be treasure troves. He even persuaded Raymond to accompany him on one of these archeological expeditions. Glass insulators were another, related, interest. These were most often found along abandoned railroad tracks, where telegraph lines used to run. And of course there were always arrowheads to hunt for.

With all these diggings, these delvings into the past, to keep him occupied, the Thompson screenhouse with its incumbent ghost could wait.

By the time October came around Christopher was able to convince himself that, since he was unlikely to learn anything more about the ghost, he should drop the subject entirely, both from conversation and from thought. After all, the nightmares though bothersome were preferable to ridicule from his friends, or worse, whatever he might encounter, alone, in the screenhouse.

Quite unexpectedly, Christopher's father was given a promotion by the company he worked for that required relocation out of state. Though they waited until the end of the school year before actually moving, Christopher's parents put their house up for sale, and the matter of the ghost, with the attendant nightmares, became moot.

❧

It wasn't until many years later that for some reason—if asked he would have been hard pressed to explain why, exactly—Christopher found himself back in Massachusetts in the vicinity of the old family homestead. Perhaps it was his recent divorce that sent him wandering, perhaps something else. As a young boy he had gone out into the woods to poke around and dig up things from the past: old bottles, glass insulators, Indian relics. Now in late middle age he was once again digging, in his mind, though, for memories rather than objects. The most arcane memory, the one he delved deepest for, but which when unearthed required no mental rinsing off or other cleansing, was that of the haunted screenhouse.

It wasn't the old homestead, therefore, that he sought out on his pilgrimage home; it was the old Thompson screenhouse.

He drove there without having to ask directions, over roads which despite decades of residential and commercial development looked familiar enough. In no time at all he found the dirt track: overgrown with weeds, though not more so than on his previous visit, when because of the presence of the bog workers he had turned around and gone home. In fact, in the intervening years not much about the bog or the screenhouse had changed. The hand pump was still there, rusted almost to nothing now, a memorial to antiquated technology; the pipe to which it was attached entered the ground at an angle, suggesting that a truck or other vehicle had backed into it and partially dislodged it.

Even though it was September, with harvest season approaching, the bog was deserted. Well that made sense. It was, after all, Sunday. Even bog workers get a day off occasionally.

As he had done so many years ago as a boy, he circumambulated the screenhouse, twice, as if that were a magical number. The windows, opaque with grime, were still intact, every one of them. Did the ghost, by its very presence, preserve the building and keep it safe from all harm?

There appeared to be no locks on the doors. But hadn't all the doors been firmly secured that other time when he and his friend Raymond—who had told him about the ghost in the first place—tried, halfheartedly, to enter? Perhaps it was merely their lack of determination, and nothing so mundane as locks on doors, that had kept them out.

A door to the rear of the screenhouse, the first he tried, yielded readily to his touch. He hardly twisted the knob, hardly exerted pressure. And yet the door swung inward, as if he were being encouraged to set aside inhibitions about private property and step inside. He did so, closing the door behind him. If asked why, given the building's reputation (and the nightmares that had so troubled him as a child), he did not leave the door wide open, he would have said that he was no longer afraid. Had in fact never been afraid.

To have left the door open, even slightly ajar, would have been to invite fear to enter with him.

Filtered through the layers of grime that coated the windows, the late afternoon sun provided scant light. Within the screenhouse it was neither night nor day but rather a murky twilight. He could see objects, such as stacks of wooden bushel boxes (which further obstructed the light) and antiquated machinery once used to harvest the berries or cull the bad from the good, but not clearly. Heated by the meager afternoon light that did manage to enter, the trapped air felt heavy, oppressive, alive only with the dust motes his movements stirred.

Nothing else stirred. All was utter silence. So where was this specter, this spook that had so obsessed his adolescent imagination?

The answer to that question came slowly, over a matter of several hours; it crept in with the lengthening shadows of nightfall that seemed to mask, rather than drain, the light, so that his inability to see more than just a few inches beyond himself was not so much a matter of the dark as it was a sort of induced blindness.

He staggered around, not in a panic, but in the manner of one who finds himself in a strange place and explores, as best he can, his surroundings. He bumped into things. In his peregrinations throughout the cluttered room he became enmeshed in cobwebs so that he wore them like a robe, or shroud. It was at that point that he realized, finally, just who the ghost might be.

Petal on a Wet, Black Bough

The title for this next tale derives from a famous haiku by that

learned but crotchety poet Ezra Pound. A careful reading

of the story will reveal its relevance. Though the names

of the characters are entirely fictitious, the cranberry

bog on which the events occurred exists,

somewhere on Cape Cod.

"WE CREATE OUR OWN GHOSTS."

Leclair reached for his brandy, which rested on the small rectangular table between him and the fireplace. He lifted the snifter and cradled it in his hands like a chalice, as if about to make a votive offering. As he tilted the snifter to his lips flames leapt into the glass; the amber took on a ruby glow. For a moment Leclair sipped not brandy but a magic potion brewed from precious gems.

A trick of the light, of course. But it helped set the mood.

"Which isn't to say the ghosts aren't real," he added. "Oh no, they're all the more real for our having created them."

It was Christmas Eve and raining: a dull, steady downpour that dampened the holiday spirit, threatened to wash it away as completely as it had the dusting of snow that had fallen earlier in the week. Water splashing against the unshaded window that fronted the ocean formed grotesque patterns on the pane, gargoyles that leered in, mocking us with their changing shapes.

We had dined well but that was an hour ago. The weather was making us restless. McWilliams—our host that evening—got up and added a log to the fire. Sousa lighted his pipe. DiGrassi took it upon himself to replenish everyone's snifter with brandy from the cut-glass decanter, then settled back in his chair and waited for Leclair to begin.

We all seemed to agree that a good ghost story, well told, would set things right, restore balance to the season, make it seem Christmas again.

"This involves a young couple," Leclair said. "The man—let us call him Gerard—owned a number of cranberry bogs on Cape Cod. His parents died young, leaving Gerard quite well off, well off in the way some farmers are, on paper, though they have to work hard and put in long hours to realize any of that wealth. And then of course there's always the weather. But this is a ghost story, not a treatise on farming."

He glanced toward McWilliams, who had a reputation for impatience, always urging people to get on with it, though he himself was a rambler whose own tales as often as not petered out without coming to any definite conclusion. Tonight, perhaps because he was host, or perhaps because like the rest of us he felt a need for the peculiar solace a ghost story imparts—tonight McWilliams sat relaxed in his chair, a benign expression softening his usually dour countenance.

"My story begins back in the Sixties," Leclair added. "During Vietnam." Pausing, he stared into the fire.

His words had an unsettling effect. DiGrassi shifted uncomfortably in his chair. Sousa stifled a nervous cough, became impatient with his pipe and knocked it out against the hearth. We all shared memories of that era, whether we fought in Southeast Asia or actively avoided the draft or just mucked our way through adolescence into manhood. No special skills were required to conjure up demons from those turbulent times.

"Don't worry," Leclair said. "The war has little to do with my story—at least, no direct bearing. I'm just setting the scene.

"The woman—Cheryl—was a city girl. From Boston. They met while students at Boston University. Cheryl, who majored in English, was a writer, always spouting poetry, some of it her own. Her poems appeared regularly in the college newspaper. By her junior year she'd been published in a dozen literary journals, and magazines like *The Atlantic* were including favorable comments with their rejection slips.

"She was a small, wispy girl, pretty in an elfin sort of way.

"Gerard majored in history. Though his mother was dead his father was still alive. And indulgent. Gerard would eventually take over the cranberry business but in the meantime let the boy get an education, have his college fling. As it was, the father never lived to see his son graduate.

"Why did this intellectual—I almost said ethereal—young woman marry a cranberry farmer from Cape Cod? Well, to begin with he wasn't bad looking. Handsome, actually, in a rugged sort of way. All those long hot summers toiling on the bogs worked wonders for his physique.

"And then of course he worshipped her. She wasn't the first goddess to succumb to the infatuation of a mere mortal.

"So they married, and he took her home to live with him in the house he'd inherited."

"Ah, now for the haunted part," McWilliams piped in.

Leclair—engrossed in his narrative—cast a startled look at his host. Reaching for his brandy he said: "Not quite yet. No, the haunting comes later. Not much later," he added, as if to soothe an impatient child.

"The house, a two-story gambrel, was built in the 1880's. Deep in the woods—as deep as you can get on Cape Cod, which is after all a narrow peninsula. Despite all the development there are still a few isolated spots, and this was one of them.

"The house was surrounded by trees and rested on a knoll overlooking a hundred acres of cranberry bog. There were no other houses nearby."

"Ah," McWilliams said.

"Yes," Leclair agreed. "Perfect for a haunting." With a motion of his hand he declined DiGrassi's offer of more brandy.

"Well, here's what happened. They'd married in June, right after graduation, a busy time in the cranberry industry: weeds and insects to control, fertilizers to apply, drought to contend with.

"Cheryl took over management of the household: vacuuming and dusting, doing laundry, shopping, preparing meals. You might think it odd for a bride of the Sixties to assume the role of housewife but for Cheryl it was ideal. It gave her time to write.

"The thing that mattered most in her life was poetry. If she hadn't married Gerard she would have been compelled to take up teaching or some other equally distasteful profession. No, she was quite content to spend three or four hours on domestic chores and devote the remainder of the day to sitting at her desk by the window overlooking the bog composing poems that would make her immortal.

"That's how their lives went for the first two or three years. Like most farmers Gerard was his own boss, and a slave to the elements. In the spring and fall he'd spend entire nights away from home fighting frost. He'd make the rounds (they owned bogs in several towns) checking thermometers, starting pumps, cleaning clogged sprinkler heads, repairing broken pipelines. And leave Cheryl all alone in that house in the woods."

The rain had intensified. The wind blowing in off the ocean picked it up and slammed it against the windows. This time Leclair accepted the proffered brandy.

"Gerard had a crew working for him. Some of them had worked for his father. But most were transients; they'd stay for a season or two then drift on to the next job or wherever fate took them.

"One October evening the phone rang. It was the State Agricultural Station with a frost warning. Cheryl took the message—the predicted minimum temperature, the tolerance of the berries, the likelihood of the wind picking up toward morning.

"'Doesn't sound too bad,' she said, wrapping her arms around her husband. 'Can't you skip tonight?'

"But of course he couldn't, with thousands of dollars worth of berries at stake. 'If the wind does pick up I should be home early—no later than three,' he promised.

"'I may take in a movie,' Cheryl said. 'I haven't been out of the house in weeks.'

"They kissed, and he changed into work clothes and left.

"There was a definite nip in the air. Overhead the stars hung remote, as if frozen in black ice. All the signs pointed to a dangerous frost.

"As he climbed into his pickup he noticed that Cheryl's green Dodge had a scratch on the passenger's side. He made a mental note to mention it in the morning. The dirt road leading from the house didn't become paved until after it skirted the bog, just before crossing a narrow wooden bridge that spanned the nearby river. Gerard had fallen behind in his maintenance; the vegetation needed trimming. The car had probably scraped against an encroaching branch."

Leclair paused and some of us took the opportunity to visit the bathroom. McWilliams, still the perfect host, heaped chunks of wood on the fire. The rain was coming down with a vengeance now; the wind if anything was growing stronger. The chimney had an exceptional flue; hardly any smoke was driven back into the room. What little smoke there was came from Sousa's pipe.

"There *was* a frost that night," Leclair said. "A bad one. Gerard was out all night manning the pumps. He wasn't able to shut them off until just before dawn.

"When at last he nosed the pickup onto the lane that led toward the house he saw the sun lifting above the tree line, a flaming orb splashing liquid fire over the unpicked berries. During the night water sprayed from the sprinkler heads had frozen as it drenched the weeds that poked here and there through the vines, creating thousands of ice statues. The sun's rays striking the sculpted crystal transformed it into sparkling gold.

"Eager to wake Cheryl so that she could share in the dazzling beauty Gerard sped along the winding road. But even as he stepped on the gas he knew he'd be too late. By the time he reached the house and roused his wife from bed the sun would have fully risen and the ice-coated weeds would have lost their breathless magic in the ordinary light of day.

"When he reached the narrow wooden bridge he saw the smashed railing and below, in the swirling eddies, the top of his wife's Dodge thrusting through the surface like the carapace of a giant turtle. And knew that he was too late, forever.

"He slammed his foot on the brake, scrambled out of the pickup and leapt over the side of the bridge as if haste were imperative—when of course the accident must have occurred hours ago.

"He hit the frigid water and immediately touched bottom. The current was sluggish and he was able to half wade, half swim over to the automobile.

"The water though murky was clear enough for him to see that she was still inside. Frantically—as if time made a difference—he yanked at the door but it had jammed and wouldn't budge. He worked his way around to the passenger side, the door of which had sprung open, and at some risk to his own life was able to pull her free from the driver's seat. Her hair, which she'd always worn long, tangled in the steering wheel but eventually he got her out. Without too much difficulty he managed to convey her body to shore where he collapsed and sobbing held her in his arms.

"Well," Leclair said, looking up from the fireplace, which he'd been staring into as if viewing the scene in its flames, "I told you this was a ghost story and I suppose you're impatient for the ghost to appear.

"It was seven or eight weeks after the accident. Gerard was returning home for the evening—it was December, a night like this except the rain was turning to snow: gross, soggy flakes that flitted into the swath cut by his headbeams like tiny albino bats, making the road slick with their slime.

"You can see that his thoughts were morbid. Since Cheryl's death he had thrown himself into a frenzy of work. He spent his days on the bogs building dikes, repairing flumes, cutting and burning brush—anything to numb his body and deaden his brain with fatigue.

"The police had investigated and come to the conclusion that Cheryl, returning from the movies, had lost control of the car—the temperature dipped below freezing that night; spray from the sprinklers might have drifted onto the road creating an icy patch; or she might have fallen asleep at the wheel or swerved to avoid an animal—and plunged into the river, been knocked unconscious, and drowned.

"At first there had been some suspicion of foul play. One of the bog workers, a drifter named Brad Pearson, disappeared the night of the accident. There was speculation that he might have been involved in Cheryl's death. But since there wasn't any evidence, or any reason beside his sudden disappearance to link him with the incident—and also because it came to light that he was a draft evader with good reason to keep on the move—for all these reasons the police dropped Pearson from their investigation and accepted the obvious, that Cheryl had died by innocent, if tragic, means.

"Returning home through the storm, preoccupied with his thoughts, Gerard was confronted by an apparition: a luminous shape that materializing from the swirling snow loomed suddenly before his windshield in the center of the bridge from which his wife had plunged to her death.

"Though indistinct the thing had human contours and seemed to be waving its arms as if signaling him to stop.

"Gerard swerved and the truck skidded. He managed to keep control though the right fender scraped against the newly repaired railing and he came within inches of spinning around. The apparition vanished as suddenly as it had appeared.

"Badly shaken, Gerard attributed the experience to his overwrought mind and drove on home. As he swung into the driveway his headlights glanced off the side of the house and there, in the illumination, he saw it distinctly: a phantom form—Cheryl!—peering through the window as if awaiting his return.

"He dashed into the house. He had reached that level of grief, you see, where he would have embraced his wife in any form, however foul, even had her rotting corpse lifted itself from the grave to crawl home to him.

"He was greeted, not by the revenant of his wife, but by the stillness of an empty house. He rushed from room to room like a madman shouting her name, pleading with her to show herself so that he might enfold her in his arms.

"He encountered only the hollow mockery of his desperate cries.

"But oh, it had been Cheryl, he was sure of that! He could close his eyes and see her: the dear familiar face upon which he had bestowed a million kisses, white with the pallor of death, enveloped in an aureole of flowing hair black with a sheen pure as unblemished onyx, framed by the window where she sat dreaming her poems, gazing out over the acres of bog awaiting his return.

"In a daze he prepared and consumed a hasty supper, then devoted himself to the evening's task. In going through Cheryl's effects he had come across a bundle of poems written in the last few months of her life. Untyped, scrawled in pencil on cheap composition paper and gathered together with a rubber band, they were unlike anything she had written before.

"Cheryl's earlier poems were good and had showed promise of greatness. In these later poems the promise had been realized; she had found her voice. Richly sensual, erotic even, they wrenched the language of love into convolutions never before seen in American poetry. Gerard was determined to see that they got published.

"That evening he began the task of typing them. As he typed he was struck by the intensity of the poems, their raw emotion, their expression of physical love—as though Cheryl, slumbering through two years of marriage, had suddenly awakened to sexual passion.

"He worked late into the night. As he got deeper into the poems he began to be troubled by a strange sensation, a feeling of guilt, as if he was somehow violating Cheryl's privacy.

"Absurd, he told himself. He was her husband. She'd want him to read the poems, see that they got published.

"Finally he went to bed. Exhausted, he fell immediately asleep. I suppose if this were a conventional ghost story his dreams would have been hagridden; he would have awakened with a start in the wee hours to mysterious sounds in the parlor. But no, he slept soundly and the following morning rose early again.

"Several inches of snow had fallen. Gerard attached a plow to his pickup, cleared his driveway and the lane leading in, then drove off to one of his distant bogs to inspect a flume that needed repair.

"He was gone all day. Remnants of the storm clung to Cape Cod.

The skies were overcast; dusk fell early. By the time he turned into the lane daylight had faded to a dull pewter. He didn't bother to snap on his headlights; he was nearly home and knew the road well.

"But when he reached the bridge he felt a sudden panic. Though his initial impulse was to speed across he forced himself to slow down. He inched the pickup over the narrow bridge, peering ahead, straining to pierce the gloom. He was afraid to turn on his lights because of what he might— or might not—see.

"He saw it anyhow: a movement of shadow, an obscure mass that rose from the water and drifted into his path where it hovered, inchoate in the dying light.

"Gerard stomped his foot on the brake pedal. As the pickup jerked to a stop he switched on the headlamps. In their beams the darkness dissolved; the road stretched away empty before him.

"He sped on home.

"There the pattern continued. He saw her—Cheryl—at the window, staring into the shadows as if *she* were the widow and he the ghost she waited for. He got out of the truck and stumbled over the lawn. As he lurched toward her she vanished and he found himself clutching at the empty pane.

"The winter passed slowly. There were days when because of the weather Gerard was unable to work outside, so he devoted himself to typing the poems, and when he had typed them, to finding a publisher. There were days when he avoided the bridge and days when he went there deliberately.

"He saw the phantom again, many times, always at night. And Cheryl, keeping vigil at the window. Gone, always, by the time he reached the house."

Leclair paused as if reluctant to go on. McWilliams went to the bar and opened a fresh bottle of brandy. Bypassing the decanter he went around and poured directly from the bottle into our snifters.

"I don't quite understand," Sousa said, relighting his pipe. "At first I thought it was Cheryl's ghost Gerard saw at the bridge. But you seem to imply there were two ghosts, Cheryl's *and* the one at the bridge."

"Oh, I got the impression there were two ghosts all along," DiGrassi said. "I assume it was the phantom at the bridge that frightened Cheryl and caused the accident." He glanced at Leclair for corroboration.

"Let Leclair tell it his own way," McWilliams said. "It's early yet; we've got plenty of time. And there's half a case of brandy in the cabinet."

"Excellent brandy, too," Leclair said.

"Well," he went on, "I'm nearly finished. That spring some boys went canoeing on the river and came upon the badly decomposed body of a man snagged in some bushes downriver from the bridge."

"Ah," DiGrassi said. "The draft evader."

Leclair nodded. "Brad Pearson, who disappeared the night Cheryl was killed."

"The sprung door?" DiGrassi inquired.

"Exactly. The police theorized that Pearson had been a passenger in the car. When it went off the bridge into the river Cheryl was trapped inside but Pearson's door was flung open by the impact and his body swept away. There was no proof, of course, but the detective in charge of the investigation suggested to Gerard that, returning home from the movies, Cheryl might have seen Pearson hitchhiking and offered him a ride. He might have made improper advances, or even attacked her, causing her to lose control of the car. The official report merely stated that both deaths were accidental.

"Gerard had his own theory. He never mentioned seeing the ghosts, of course. But there were those poems, you see. He had felt all along that *he* hadn't inspired their passion."

"Cheryl was carrying on with Pearson," DiGrassi said. "Tell me, did Gerard ever get the poems published?"

Leclair shook his head. "No. He could have. A New York publisher was interested. But Gerard dropped the matter. The poems are tucked away in a closet in an unused room."

We sat for a while listening to the rain. Then Leclair got up to leave.

"Before you go, one more thing. The ghosts—does he still see them?" DiGrassi asked.

"Yes," Leclair said. And then he left. He owned cranberry bogs, we knew, and lived in a lonely house in the woods. We didn't envy him his long drive home.

About the Artist

PLYMOUTH ARTIST **JOYCE DIETLIN**, whose oil painting "Autumn Reflections" on the dust jacket of *Moonlight Harvest* so perfectly echoes the book's haunted themes, began painting with oils thirty years ago with Plymouth artist Samual Evans. She also took painting classes with Michael Keane, now a Cape Cod artist, and has studied at the Massachusetts College of Art in Boston.

She exhibits gallery displays at the Golden Gull Studios on the Plymouth waterfront, at Artica Gallery in Duxbury, and at My Sister's Gallery in Sandwich.